SURFING
THE GNARL

plus...

SURFING
THE GNARL

plus

"The Men in the Back Room at the Country Club"

and

"Rapture in Space"

and

"Load on the Miracles and Keep a Straight Face"
Outspoken Interview

RUDY RUCKER

PM PRESS

"The Men in the Back Room at the Country Club" appeared in *Infinite Matrix*, December 2005, and in *Mad Professor* (Thunder's Mouth Press, 2007). "Rapture in Space" appeared in *Semiotext[e] SF* (Autonomedia, 1989), and in *Gnarl!* (Four Walls Eight Windows, 2000). Some passages from "Surfing the Gnarl" appeared in *The Lifebox, the Seashell, and the Soul* (Basic Books, 2005), *Mad Professor* (Thunder's Mouth Press, 2007), and *Nested Scrolls* (PS Publishing and Tor Books, 2011).

Series Editor: Terry Bisson

ISBN: 978-1-60486-309-3
LCCN: 2011927979

PM Press
P. O. Box 23912
Oakland, CA 94623
PMPress.org

Printed in the USA on recycled paper, by the Employee Owners of Thomson-Shore in Dexter, Michigan
www.thomsonshore.com

Outsides: John Yates/Stealworks.com
Insides: Josh MacPhee/Justseeds.org

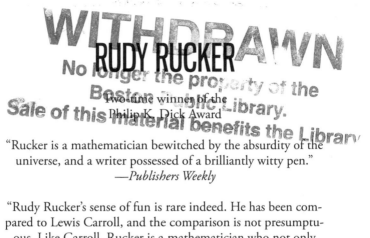

RUDY RUCKER

Two-time winner of the
Philip K. Dick Award

"Rucker is a mathematician bewitched by the absurdity of the universe, and a writer possessed of a brilliantly witty pen."
—*Publishers Weekly*

"Rudy Rucker's sense of fun is rare indeed. He has been compared to Lewis Carroll, and the comparison is not presumptuous. Like Carroll, Rucker is a mathematician who not only enjoys paradoxes, but can propagate that enjoyment as pure lunatic humor."
—*Washington Post*

"Reading a Rudy Rucker book is like finding Poe, Kerouac, Lewis Carroll and Philip K. Dick parked in your driveway in a topless '57 Caddy . . . and telling you they're taking you for a RIDE. The funniest science fiction author around."
—*Sci-Fi Universe*

"Rudy Rucker is an oddity and a treasure."
—*Wired*

"Rucker's sensibility is a combination of gonzo humor, fictionalized autobiography in the Kerouacian mode (what Rucker calls 'transrealism'), and the sheer, bugs-in-your-teeth thrill of scientific extrapolation taken to blitz-punk extremes."
—*Salon.com*

"Rucker's writing is great like the Ramones are great: a genre stripped to its essence, attitude up the wazoo. . . . No one does the cyber version of beatnik glory quite like Rucker."
—*NY Review of Science Fiction*

PM PRESS OUTSPOKEN AUTHORS SERIES

CONTENTS

THE MEN IN THE BACK ROOM AT THE COUNTRY CLUB

"YO, JACK," SAID TONEL as they lugged two golf bags apiece toward the men's locker room. It was sunset, the end of a long Saturday's caddying, Jack's last day of work this summer.

"I didn't get a chance to tell you," continued Tonel, shouldering open the door. "About who I saw sweatin' in Ragland's backyard this morning." It was fresh and cool in the locker room. A nice break from the heavy, thick August air.

"In Ragland's yard?" said Jack Vaughan, setting down the bags and wiping his brow. "I don't know. His ninety-year-old mother?" Jack suspected a joke. Ragland was the master of the locker room, ensconced behind his counter. Tidily cleaned shoes and piles of fresh white towels sat on the white-painted shelves around him. Although the bare-skulled Ragland's eyes were half-closed, it was likely that he was listening.

"It was the five mibracc," said Tonel. "Doin' Ragland's yard work. Isn't that right, Ragland? What's the dealio? How you get to slave-driving them Republicans?

I need to know." Tonel lived right next door to Ragland. The two weren't particularly fond of each other.

"Don't be mouthin' on my business, yellow dog," said Ragland. Though he cleaned the shoes of popinjays, he insisted on his dignity.

A burst of talk echoed from the little back room beyond Ragland's station. Just like every other morning or afternoon, the mibracc—the caddies' nickname for "men in the back room at the country club"—were in there, safe from women, out of the daylight, playing cards and drinking the bourbon they stored in their lockers.

"Those bagworts do chores?" said Jack. "No way, Tonel."

"I seen it," insisted Tonel. "Mr. Atlee was draggin' a plow with Mr. Early steerin' it. Mr. Gupta was down on his knees pullin' up weeds, and Mr. Inkle and Mr. Cuthbert was carryin' trash out to the alley. Ole Ragland sittin' on the back porch with his shotgun across his knees. Did your Meemaw put conjure on them, Ragland?"

"You want me to snapify your ass?" said Ragland. Though gray and worn, Ragland was, in his own way, an imposing man.

Tonel made a series of mystic passes, hoodoo signs, and rap gestures in Ragland's direction.

"I'll ask the men myself," said Jack, caught up by Tonel's rebellious spirit.

The two boys stepped into the back room, a plain space with a tile floor and shiny green paint on the windowless concrete walls. The five old men sat in battered wooden captain's chairs around a table from the club's lounge. Oily Mr. Atlee was dealing out cards to spindly, white-haired Mr. Early, to bald-as-a-doorknob Mr. Inkle, to Mr. Cuthbert with his alarming false teeth, and to Mr. Gupta, the only nonwhite member of the Killeville Country Club.

"Hi, guys," said Jack.

There was no response. The mibracc studied their cards, sipping at their glasses of bourbon and water, their every little gesture saying, "Leave us alone." Mr. Inkle stubbed out a cigarette and lit a fresh one.

"Listen up," said Tonel in a louder tone. "I gotta axe you gentlemen somethin'. Was you bustin' sod for Ragland today? My friend here don't believe me."

Still no answer. The mibracc were so fully withdrawn into their clubby little thing that you could just as well try talking to your TV. Or to five spiteful children.

"Scoop," grunted Mr. Cuthbert, standing up with his glass in hand. Mr. Gupta handed him his empty glass as well. With the slightest grunt of nonrecognition, Mr. Cuthbert sidled past Tonel and Jack, moving a little oddly, as if his knees were double-jointed. His oversized plastic teeth glinted in the fluorescent light. Mr. Cuthbert pressed his thumb to his locker's pad, opened the door, and dipped the two glasses down into his golf bag. Jack could smell the bourbon, a holiday smell.

The mibracc's golf bags held no clubs. They were lined with glass, with tall golf bag–sized glass beakers, or carboys. Big glass jars holding gallons of premium bourbon. It was a new gimmick, strictly hush-hush; nobody but Ragland and the caddies knew. Mr. Atlee, a former druggist, had obtained the carboys, and Mr. Early, a former distiller's rep, had arranged for a man to come one night with an oak cask on a dolly to fill the bags. The mibracc were loving it.

Mr. Cuthbert shuffled back past Tonel toward the card table, the liquid swirling in his two glasses. The boy fell into step behind the old man, draping his hand onto the mibracc's shoulder. Mr. Cuthbert paid him no mind. Jack joined the procession, putting his hand on Tonel's shoulder and trucking along in his friend's wake. Tonel was humming the chorus of the new video by Ruggy Qaeda, the part with the zombies machine-gunning the yoga class.

After Mr. Cuthbert dropped into his chair and picked up his cards, Jack and Tonel circled the room two, three, four times, with Tonel finally bursting into song. Never did the mibracc give them a second glance. Odd as it seemed, the liquid in the glasses still hadn't settled down; it was moving around as if someone were stirring it.

Around then Ragland came out from behind his counter, wielding a wet, rolled-up towel. Silly as it sounded, being snapped by the old locker room attendant was a serious threat. Ragland was the ascended kung-fu master of the towel snap. He could put a bruise on your neck that would last six weeks. Laughing and whooping, Tonel and Jack ran outside.

A white face peered out of the window in the clubhouse's terrace door. The door swung open and a plain, slightly lumpish girl in a white apron appeared. Gretchen Karst.

"I'm pregnant, Jack," said Gretchen, her sarcastic, pimply face unreadable. "Marry me tonight. Take me off to college with you tomorrow."

"How do you know it's me?" protested Jack. "I'm not the only—I mean even Tonel said he—"

"Tonel is a horn worm. All I gave him was a hand job. And it didn't take very long. Jack, there's a justice of the peace out on Route 501. Ronnie Blevins. He works at Rash Decisions Tattoo. I found him online. Since it's Saturday, they're open till midnight. I'm off work right now, you know. I started early today."

"Stop it, Gretchen. You and me—it's not—"

"I'm serious," said Gretchen, although there was in fact a good chance that she was scamming him. Gretchen had a twisted mind. "You're my best chance, Jack," she continued. "Marry me and take me with you. I'm smart. I like sex. And I'm carrying your son."

"Uh—"

Just then someone shouted for Gretchen from the corner of the clubhouse building. It was Gretchen's dad, standing at the edge of the parking lot. He'd trimmed his flattop to high-tolerance precision and he was wearing his shiny silver jogging suit. All set for the weekly meeting at the Day Six Synod's tabernacle.

Gretchen could talk about the Day Six Synod for hours. It was a tiny splinter religion based on the revelation that Armageddon, the last battle, was coming one-seventh sooner than the Seventh Day Adventists had thought. We were already in the end times, in fact, with the last act about to be ushered in by manifestations of Shekinah Glory, this being the special supernatural energy that God—and Satan—use to manifest themselves. The pillar of fire that led the Israelites to the promised land, the burning bush that spake to Moses—these had been Shekinah Glory. The Day Six Synod taught that our Armageddon's Shekinah Glory would take the form of evil UFOs pitted against winged angels.

Karl Karst's jogging suit was silver to remind him of the Shekinah Glory. The Day Six Synod meetings featured impressively high-end computer graphics representing the Glory in its good and evil forms. Though Mr. Karst was but a county school-bus mechanic, some of the core founders of the Day Six Synod were crackpot computer hackers.

"Shake a leg or we'll be late," shouted Mr. Karst. "Hi, Jack and Tonel. Wait till you see who I've got with me, Gretchen!"

"I'll deal with you later," said Gretchen to Jack with a slight smile. Surely she'd only been teasing him about the pregnancy. She made the telephone gesture with her thumb and pinky. "We'll coordinate."

"Okay," said Jack, walking with her toward her father. "I'm visualizing hole six." Hole six of the KCC golf course was the popular place for the club's young workers to party. It was well away from the road, on a hillock surrounded on three sides by kudzu-choked woods.

Right now, Jack figured to eat dinner at Tonel's. He didn't want to go to his own house at all. Because this morning on the way to the Killeville Country Club, he'd doubled back home, having forgotten his sunglasses, and through the kitchen window he'd seen his mom kissing the Reverend Doug Langhorne.

It wasn't all that surprising that Doug Langhorne would make a play for the tidy, crisp widow Jessie Vaughan, she of the cute figure, tailored suits, and bright lipstick. Jessie was the secretary for the shabby-genteel St. Anselm's Episcopal Church on a once-grand boulevard in downtown Killeville, right around the corner from the black neighborhood where Tonel lived, not that any black people came to St. Anselm's. Jessie's salary was so meager that Reverend Langhorne let Jessie and Jack live with him in the rectory, a timeworn Victorian manse right next to the church.

Doug Langhorne's wife and children shared the rectory as well. Lenore Langhorne was a kind, timid soul, nearsighted, overweight and ineffectual, a not-so-secret drinker of cooking sherry, and the mother of four demanding unattractive children dubbed with eminent Killeville surnames. Banks, Price, Sydnor, and Rainey Langhorne.

Setting down his bicycle and stepping up onto his home's porch this morning, Jack had seen his mother in a lip lock with Doug Langhorne. And then Mom had seen Jack seeing her. And then, to make it truly stomach-churning, Jack had seen Lenore and her children in the shadows of the dining room, witnessing the kiss as well. The couple broke their clinch; Jack walked in and took his sunglasses; Lenore let out a convulsive sob; Doug cleared his throat and said, "We have to talk."

"Daddy kissed Jack's mommy!" cried Banks Langhorne, a fat little girl with a low forehead. Her brother Rainey and her sisters Price and Sydnor took up the cry. "Daddy's gonna get it, Daddy's gonna get it, Daddy's gonna get it . . ." There was something strange about the children's ears; they were pointed at the tips, like the ears of devils or of pigs. The children joined hands in a circle around Doug and Jessie and began dancing a spooky Ring-Around-the-Rosie. Lenore was trying to talk through her racking sobs. Doug was bumblingly trying to smooth things over. Mom was looking around the room with an expression of distaste, as if wondering how she'd ended up here. On the breakfast table, the juice in the children's glasses was unaccountably swirling, as if there were a tiny whirlpool in each. Jack rushed outside, jumped on his bike, and rode to work, leaving the children's chanting voices behind.

Jack had pretty much avoided thinking about it all day, and what should he think anyway? It was Jessie's business who she kissed. And surely he'd only imagined the pointed ears on those dreadful piggy children. But what about Lenore? Although Lenore was like a dusty stuffed plush thing that made you sneeze, she was nice. She'd always been good to Jack. Her sob was maybe the saddest thing he'd ever heard. Grainy, desperate, hopeless, deep. What did the kiss mean for Mom's future as the church secretary? What did it bode for Doug Langhorne's position as rector? What a mess.

Jack's plan was to stay out most of the night or all of the night with his friends, grab his suitcase in the morning, and get the 8:37 a.m. bus to Virginia Polytechnic Institute in Blacksburg. And there he'd begin his real life. Let Mom and Lenore and Doug work things out in pawky, filthy Killeville. Jack's bag was packed. He was ready to set off for the great outer world!

With these thoughts running in his head, he followed Gretchen to the parking lot, Tonel tagging along. Mr. Karst was mounted in his battered secondhand Ford SUV. Sitting next to him was an unkempt, overweight, luminously white guy smoking a filter cigarette.

"Albert Chesney!" exclaimed Gretchen.

"Him!" said Jack. The thirty-year-old Albert Chesney was a Day Six Synodite and a convicted computer criminal. He'd just gotten parole; his release had been a topic in the *Killeville Daily News* for several days. Three years ago, Chesney had brought down the entire Internet for a week with his infamous <endtimes> e-mail, which had combined the nastiest features of spam, hypnotism, a virus, a pyramid scheme, a con-game, a worm, and a denial-of-service attack. At the cost of infecting seven hundred million machines, <endtimes> had netted seven converts to the Day Six Synod.

"Don't ride with him, Gretchen," said Jack, suddenly visualizing a defenseless big-eyed fetus within Gretchen's slightly curved belly. He seemed to recall that Chesney had always been interested in Gretchen. Chesney was single, with no relatives.

"Oh, now you're all protective?" said Gretchen. "Don't worry. I can handle myself. Welcome back, Albert. Are you fully rehabilitated?"

"I've hoed a long, lonely row," sighed Albert Chesney. His voice was husky; his head was big and crooked like a jack-o'-lantern. "The Pharisees say I'm not allowed to live in a house with computers. What with the Synod having the tabernacle on my farm, I'm exiled to a humble abode on Route 501. Leastways it won't be but one night. The last battle's comin' tomorrow morning, hallelujah and pass it on. Armageddon. Angels and devils fighting for the fate of our world. Drive your chariot onward, Karl. I need a taste of my sweet country roads. And then I'll prophesy to the fellowship about the Shekinah Glory."

"You bet, Albert," said Mr. Karst. "Don't he look good, Gretchen?" Mr. Karst liked Chesney because he'd let Day Six use his farmhouse for their tabernacle the whole time he'd been in jail. Swaying and backfiring, the rusty SUV lumbered off.

"Do he say the world ends tomorrow?" asked Tonel.

"Don't worry," said Jack. "They always say that. Back in May, Mr. Karst tried to stop Gretchen from buying a prom dress because the last battle was due to come before our graduation."

Turning back to the clubhouse, Tonel and Jack encountered muscular Danny Dank, who'd just finished setting up the giant propane-fueled two-whole-hog barbeque wagon that the club used for their galas. Tomorrow was the day of the club's annual Killeville Barbeque Breakfast Golf Classic, starting near dawn.

Danny tightened down the cover of the quilted chrome wagon and unwrapped a stick of marijuana gum, the pricey brand called Winnipeg Wheelchair. Grinning and chewing, he gestured for the two caddies to sit down with him on a low wall facing the eighteenth green and the last glow of the sunset.

"Listen to this," said Danny, pulling a folded up newspaper from his hip pocket. He hawked some spit on to the ground, then read, more mellifluously than one might have expected. Danny had gone to C. T. Piggott High School the same as Jack and Tonel; he'd been a senior when they'd been freshmen. But he'd been expelled before his graduation.

"Falwell County's most notorious computer criminal is temporarily lodged in the Casa Linda Motel on Highway 501 southeast of Killeville, next to a tattoo parlor and a liquor store that rents adult videos," read Danny. "His neighbors include a few parolees and at least one registered sex offender. His second-floor room in the thirty-four-unit motel overlooks the parking lot of a strip club."

"Punkin-head Chesney," said Tonel. "We just seen him. He and Gretchen goin' to church."

"Gretchen?" parroted Danny, as if unwilling or unable to understand. He was intent on his presentation. "Do you dogs grasp why I read you the news item?"

"Because you're spun," said Jack, laughing.

"Give me a piece of that gum."

"Three dollars," said Danny, reaching into shirt pocket. "Casa Linda is my crib. The county thinks they can just dump any old trash on my doorstep. I been planning to write a letter to the paper. But—"

"Who's the sex offender, Dank-man?" interrupted Tonel.

Danny looked embarrassed and chewed his gum in silence. The sex offender living at the Casa Linda was Danny. He'd been expelled from Piggott High for putting a Web cam into the girls' locker room. One of the girls who'd been showering there was frosh Lucy Candler, the pluperfect cheer daughter of Judge Bowen Candler and his wife Burke. The Judge had thrown the book at Danny. Racketeering and child pornography. Even though, Danny being Danny, the Web site hadn't worked.

"Here's three bucks," said Jack, pulling the singles out of his wallet. "This is my last night in town, Danny. Disable me, dog."

"I'm on the boat," said Tonel, getting out his own wallet.

"I'm up for a power run," said Danny, taking the money and fishing out two sticks of gum. "But Les Trucklee says I gotta be here at dawn for the barbeque. All I do in that kitchen is, like, fry frozen fries for freezing. I can't hack no more of that today. Tomorrow will be here soon enough. You dogs got any booze?"

"We know where there's a lot of bourbon," said Jack, impishly curious to see what might happen if he encouraged Danny. "Right, Tonel?" Ragland had fiercely enjoined the caddies to keep mum about the mibracc's lockers, but tonight of all nights, Jack could afford to be reckless. "You get Ragland to chasing you, Tonel," continued Jack. "And I'll scoop into Mr. Cuthbert's stash." Anything was better than going home.

"What stash?" asked Danny.

So he told Danny, and they talked it over a little more as the light faded, in no rush to actually do anything yet, the three of them chewing their Winnipeg Wheelchair. They strolled into the patch of rough between the first tee and the eighteenth green. There was a grassy dell in among the trees where they could stretch out without anyone coming along to boss them.

"Danny!"

It was the voice of Les Trucklee, the personnel manager. The boys could see him standing on the flood-lit terrace next to the barbeque wagon. He wasn't a bad guy—he'd hired Danny despite his record. Les Trucklee was gay, not too bright, in his thirties, a wannabe yup-pie, with thinning blond hair in a comb-over. He had very large ears and a fruity voice.

"Oh, Danny!" repeated Trucklee, peering out into the night. "I need you. I know you're out there! I hear your voice. You're making things hard, Danny."

Jack or Tonel could have made a lewd joke then, based on the obvious fact that Les had a crush on Danny, and on the rumored likelihood that the two were having an affair. But they knew better than to tease their older friend about so delicate a topic. Danny could turn mighty mean. And he carried a sizable pocket knife. Finally Trucklee went back inside.

"Let's get that bourbon," said Danny, breaking the strained silence.

Circling around behind the barbeque wagon, the

three made their way toward the locker room door. It had a sliding dead bolt on the outside so nobody could get out, but it had a keyed lock as well. Danny undid the bolt, but the doorknob wouldn't turn. And they hadn't even seen Ragland and the mibracc go out.

"I know another way in," said Danny. "Through the ceiling of the furnace room. You can hop up through a hole I found."

"Go in the ceiling?" said Tonel.

"There's a crawlspace," said Danny. "It goes to the ladies' locker room. There's a grate over their showers. The men's is the same."

"You're still peeping?" said Jack, a balloon of mirth rising in his chest. "You really are a sex offender, Danny. Keep it up, and the Man's gonna cut out your balls and give you Neuticles. For the public good."

"Laugh it up, bagwort," shot back Danny. "Meanwhile Albert Chesney's off with your girl."

Climbing into the ceiling was a dumb idea, but, hey. It was the end of summer. So yeah, they snuck to the furnace room, got up into the ceiling, and made their way across the hanging supports. Danny kept making snorting noises like a wild pig, and then Tonel would say "Neuticles," and then they'd laugh so hard they'd flop around like fish. They were riding the Wheelchair for fair.

Eventually they found themselves above the ceiling vent in the shower room of the men's lockers. There were voices coming up. Ragland and the mibracc. Still in here after all.

Peeking through the grate, Jack saw Ragland in the shower with the old men, all of them naked. The men looked sluggish and tired. One of them—Mr.

Gupta—had collapsed to the floor and looked oddly flat. Just now Ragland was pulling something like a cork out of Mr. Inkle's navel. A flesh-colored bung. A stream of straw-colored fluid gushed out of the mibracc, splashing on the tile floor and running toward the drain.

"Smeel," whispered Danny.

"You mean lymph," murmured Jack.

"No, dog, that's smeel," hissed Tonel. "The Dank-man knows."

They were trying to act like what they were seeing was funny—but they were realizing it wasn't. It was awful. The air smelled of urine and alcohol, meat and feces. It would be very bad if Ragland found them watching. There was no more joking, no more chat. The boys peered through the grate in silence.

Actually the smeel wasn't all running down the drain. The smelly dregs were sliding away, but a clear, sparkling fraction of the smeel was gathering in pools and eddies near the drain, humping itself up into tiny waterspouts, circling around and around, the smaller vortices joining into bigger ones. A spinning ring of smeel slid across the tiles like a miniature hurricane. It headed right out of the shower stall and disappeared into the locker room.

Meanwhile Mr. Inkle flopped over onto his side like a deflating balloon. Ragland pushed the skin around with his bare feet, then trod along its length, squeezing out the last gouts of smeel. He nudged the Inkle skin over next to the Gupta skin. After draining the three other mibracc—none of whom seemed to mind—he wrapped the five skins into tight rolls, and went out into the locker room. The clarified smeel gathered into five watery columns like miniature typhoons and followed him.

The boys heard a rattling of locker doors. The mibracc skins waited, their edges twitching ever so slightly. Ragland reappeared, still naked. He fetched the skins one by one, clattering and splashing in the next room. Each time they saw Ragland, there was one less smeel tornado following him. Evidently he was stashing the mibracc and their smeel inside the golf bags.

Next Ragland took a long, soapy shower. Then came the rustling of him getting dressed, followed by the unlocking and locking of the outer door. All was silent.

Danny lifted loose the grate and the boys dropped down onto the tiled shower room floor. Jack happened to know that under his counter Ragland had a thing like a monster Swiss knife of plastic thumbs, one thumb for each club member—in case someone died of old age, which happened often enough to matter. Jack fetched the master thumbs and opened up Mr. Cuthbert's locker. They peered into the golf bag.

Something twitched in the golden liquid, making a tiny splash. Yes. Mr. Cuthbert was in there, rolled up like a pickled squid. The preservative fluid was just level with the golf bag's top edge.

Danny leaned over and sucked up some of it.

"Yaaar," he said, wiping his lips. "Good."

The stuff seemed to hit him right away, and very hard. When he unsteadily ducked down to drink some more, his chin banged into the bag and, oh God, the bag fell over. Although the glass in the bag didn't shatter, the liquid slopped across the floor.

Mr. Cuthbert slid right out the bag, looking like a wet burrito. Tonel yanked the golf bag upright, but Mr. Cuthbert remained on the tiles.

The spilled liquor and smeel puddled around the mibracc. Slowly the fluid began eddying again, bulging itself into a mound. The stuff had shed its excremental odors in the showers. The room filled with the heady fruitcake-and-eggnog perfume of bourbon. Crazy Danny found an empty glass and dipped it into the vortex.

"Naw, naw," said Tonel, still holding the golf bag. "Don't be drinkin' that mess!"

"'S good," repeated Danny, gesturing with his glass. His pupils were crazed pinpoints. There was no reasoning with him. His Adam's apple pumped up and down as he drank.

Jack found a mop and nudged the weirdly animated smeel-bourbon into a bucket that he poured back into the golf bag. All the while the coiled skin of Mr. Cuthbert was slowly twisting around, making a peevish hissing noise.

"Help me jam him back in and let's get out of here," Jack told Tonel.

"You be touchin' him," said Tonel. "Not me."

Jack hunkered down and took hold of Mr. Cuthbert. The mibracc felt like incompletely cured food, like a half-dried apricot: leathery on the outside, wet and squishy in the middle. He was hissing louder than before. A little more smeel trickled from the bunghole in his belly-button.

Gritting his teeth, Jack rerolled Mr. Cuthbert and slid him into his golf bag. The skin twitched and splashed. A drop of the bourbon-smeel landed on Jack's lower lip. Reflexively he licked it off. Error. The room began ever so slowly to spin.

While Jack paused, assessing the damages, crazy Danny reached past him to scoop out one last glassful of the poison bourbon. Mr. Cuthbert's golf bag rocked and clattered; bubbles rose to the surface. The noises echoed back from the other mibracc. All five lockers were shaking.

"Let's bounce," urged Tonel, over by the locker room door. He already had it open, he'd unlocked the doorknob lock. And they'd left the outside dead bolt open.

"There you are, Danny," came the voice of Les Trucklee as they stepped out onto the floodlit terrace. He was out there checking over the barbeque wagon and smoking a cigarette. "I hope I'm not seeing what I think I'm seeing in your hand."

Jack quickly closed the locker room door behind them. He didn't bother fastening the manual bolt. Surely the mibracc couldn't get out of their lockers unaided.

"You ain't seein' squat," Danny was saying, holding the glass behind his back. "I gotta leave now, Les, I just got a message from my boys here. It's my mother. She's real sick."

"Mother Dank ill again?" said Les in an indulgent, disbelieving tone. "She's a susceptible old dear, isn't she? Maybe she should wear more clothes. Are you in any condition to drive, Danny? If you'll linger a bit, I could give you a lift."

"No, Les," said Danny, his voice cold. A long moment passed. Dazzled moths were beating around the lights. Dizzy from his marijuana gum and the drop of mibracc fluid, Jack was seeing glowing trails in the air behind the insects. He thought he could hear hammering sounds from the locker room, but nobody else was noticing.

"All right then," said Les, stubbing out his butt. "I'm back to serving our patrons. The ladies are on their dessert drinks, flirting with each others' husbands. They're excited about the barbeque and golf tournament tomorrow. Don't forget you're onstage bright and early, Danny, we'll want to start up the grill at the crack of dawn. You and your friends stay out of trouble tonight." Les sighed and ran his fingers through his thinning hair. "I wish I was young again. I never had enough fun."

One of the moths landed on Jack's hand. The feathery touch grated on his tautened nerves. As he brushed the moth away, he seemed to hear a faint cry, and when he glanced down he saw that the moth had a tiny head resembling that of a round-eyed woman with tangled blond hair. Jack's stifled exclamation turned Les Trucklee's attention to him.

"Good luck at college, Jack. If one of you fellows happens to get a wild hair up your ass, stop by around one or two tonight and I'll give you a free nightcap. Top shelf. Why don't you sleep on my office couch again tonight, Danny, just to be getting up early. It'll be even better than last time."

This was too much for Tonel, who let out a loud guffaw.

And then they were in the parking lot, Danny sitting on his obese black Harley gunning it. His face was dark and angry. Les had gone too far, told too much. Danny roared the motorcycle even harder.

Danny had gotten the hog used from a Killeville insurance salesman who'd bought it as a temporary stopgap against his midlife crisis before moving on to a girlfriend in Virginia Beach. The machine was loaded with puffy middle-aged accessories, including enormous hard-shelled saddlebags. Instead of tearing them off—hell, he'd paid for them, hadn't he?—Danny had gotten one of his buddies at Rash Decisions Tattoo to paint them with renditions of the Pig Chef—two smirking pigs in aprons and chef's hats, one holding a meat cleaver and the other waving a long three-tined fork with sharpness-twinkles. The Pig Chef was—if you thought about it—one of the more sinister icons of American roadside art. Danny's personal totem. What kind of pig is a butcher? What kind of pig cooks barbeque? A traitor pig, a killer pig, a doomed preterite pig destined for eternal damnation. Danny's Pig Chefs showed the full weight of this knowledge in their mocking eyes and snaggled snouts.

"I'm gonna go catch Stiffie's act," said Danny. Stiffie Ryder was his idol, his proof of masculinity, his favorite woman to peep at. Stiffie worked as a stripper at the Banana Split, a bar and grill located on the same stretch of Route 501 as the Casa Linda and Rash Decisions Tattoo, Killeville's own little Sodom and Gomorrah, just outside the city limits.

"What about those skins in the golf bags?" asked Jack. "What if they try and get out?" The drop he'd licked off his lip was still working on him. One of his legs felt shorter than the other. He put his hand on Tonel's shoulder for support.

"They can gangbang Les Trucklee," said Danny. "They can warm him up for me." He glared at Jack and Tonel, who had no thought of uttering a response. Danny brushed back his lank, greasy hair, drank off the last bit of bourbon-smeel, and tossed his glass to shatter in the parking lot. For the first time Jack noticed that the tips of Danny's ears were pointed. "I can't believe Les was talking that way in front of you two," continued Danny. "Like he's my sissy. He's gonna pay the price." And with that he roared off.

"Danny buggin' out," said Tonel. "Trucklee better watch hisself."

"I don't know how Danny can drive," said Jack. "I'm so—" He staggered to one side and puked.

"Weak bitch," said Tonel, not unkindly.

Jack heaved again, bringing up the day's four Coca-Colas and the burger and fries he'd had for lunch. Right away he felt better.

The vomit was a little heap at the edge of the asphalt, faintly lit by the terrace lights. Was it hunching itself up like the smeel had done? Beginning ever so slightly to twist into an eddy?

"Come on, dog," said Tonel. "Let's creep on home. You can pedal, can't you?"

"Yeah," said Jack, looking away from the shifting mound on the pavement. "I'm better now. I got a drop of that crap in my mouth. From the golf bags. I can't believe how much of it Danny drank. We shouldn't have let him ride."

"He'd a pulled his knife if we tried to stop him," said Tonel.

They walked over to the rack and unchained their bicycles, a couple of beat-up jobs nobody would bother to steal. The night felt thick and velvety, but it wasn't spinning anymore.

"We ought to talk to Ragland," said Jack as they pedaled off. "Ask him what's up."

"I gotta eat first," said Tonel. "Dad's makin' that burgoo."

"Can I come to your house too?" said Jack. "I don't want to go home." And then he told Tonel the story about this morning.

"That's some sad stuff," said Tonel when Jack finished. "Preachers always do like that. But you sayin' his children had pointed ears?"

"Like Danny's," sighed Jack. "Everything's coming apart, just when it's finally time for me to get out of here. Back on the terrace I thought one of those moths had a woman's head. And the mibracc—I can hardly believe we saw that. Maybe we're just really high."

"Be some mighty crunk Wheelchair make you see five men turn into somethin' like chitlins." They pedaled down Egmont Avenue in silence for a minute, the occasional car rumbling by. Jack didn't dare try and look at the drivers. Finally Tonel broke the silence. "If you not goin' by the e-rectory, how we gonna get a ride?" Normally they took Jack's mother's car out at night.

"Ask Vincente for his," said Jack.

Tonel's father Vincente ran a secondhand appliance store called Vaughan Electronics—it so happened that Tonel's and Jack's families shared the same last name, which no doubt had something to do with plantations and slaves. Sometimes Jack would tell people that Tonel was his cousin, which wasn't entirely implausible, light-skinned as Tonel was. Tonel's mother Wanda had been mostly white. Even though she'd run off to Florida, Vincente had a picture of Wanda on the kitchen wall in his apartment at the back of the store.

When the boys entered through the alley door, Vincente's wall of screens was tuned to a porno webcast; he quickly changed it to a boxing match.

"Help yourself to burgoo," said Vincente, gesturing toward the stove.

"Put the ho's back on, Daddy," said Tonel. "We don't wanna see no thugs."

"Wouldn't be fittin' to expose you," said the wiry Vincente.

He was lounging in a duct-tape-patched plastic recliner facing twenty-four clunker TVs stacked in a six by four grid. Vincente had installed special controllers so he could switch his digital mosaic between showing a bunch of random channels and showing a single channel with its image jigsawed into pieces. He'd learned electronics in the Navy during the war on Iraq. He began fiddling with his remote, breaking up and reassembling the dataflow, temporarily settling on a Sudanese dagger-fighting flick.

Meanwhile the hearty smell of the rabbit and chicken stew pushed away any lingering queasiness Jack felt. He had the munchies. He and Tonel ate quite a bit of the stew, the thuds and yelps of the movie bouncing along in the background.

Jack's smart phone rang. He peeked at the screen, fearing it would be Mom, but, no, it was Gretchen, looking tense.

"Hey," she said. "I'm still at the tabernacle. It's getting way too trippy. You think you could come and get me now?"

"Um, I guess so," said Jack. "I'm at Tonel's. We have to see about getting a car."

"Axe her can she hook me up a honey," put in Tonel. "I'm driving. Right, Daddy? I can have the van?"

"If you can start it," said Vincente, twitching his remote to break the image into twenty-four new channels. "Sneak the battery outten Ragland's truck. I seen him come back a half hour ago. You know he ain't goin' out again."

"How do you mean trippy?" Jack asked Gretchen meanwhile.

"It's that Armageddon thing," said Gretchen. There was a trumpeting noise in the background. "Albert Chesney is getting really weird about it. He wants me to spend the night with him at Casa Linda to help him 'gird his loins' for the last battle. None of the chickenshit Day Sixers wants to help him. Albert says that six pure hearts can turn the tide, so he needs five people to help him. Dad wants *me* to be with Albert even though he himself plans to stay home. Come get me, Jack. Right now they're watching a video, but when it's done, Dad plans to drive Albert and me to the Casa Linda."

"Is this another of your put-ons?"

"Save me, Jack. I mean it. And, you know, I really am pregnant." Gretchen never let up. Jack liked that about her.

"Hook me a honey," repeated Tonel.

"We're coming," said Jack. "And Tonel wants to know if you can find a date for him?"

"Pinka Wright is into him. I might call her." The trumpets rose to an off-key crescendo. "Hurry." Gretchen hung up.

The tooting noise didn't stop when Jack turned his phone off. After a moment's disorientation, he realized that Vincente had tuned his screens to some random webcast of—what was it? Three glowing donuts moving across the wall of TVs, silver, gold, and copper. Behind them was a background of unfamiliar stars. A cracked brass fanfare played. Before Jack could ask about the picture, Vincente punched his controller again, splitting the image into twenty-four new channels.

"What she say?" demanded Tonel.

"Her father wants her to spend the night with Albert Chesney," said Jack.

"She jivin' you again," said Tonel. "What she say about my date?"

"Pinka Wright."

"Ooo! Let's bounce it, dog."

"Don't let Ragland hear you," warned Vincente. "He's got that shotgun."

First of all they had to check the tires of Vincente's ancient van, and of course one of them was flat—Vincente's driving license was suspended and he didn't keep up the insurance on the van, which meant that he hardly ever drove it. Tonel found an electric pump in the bowels of Vaughan Electronics and they dragged out an extension cord and filled the tire. The tire seemed to hold its size, so that problem was solved.

Next came the issue of gas. A quick check of the van's gauge showed it to be stone cold dry. Tonel produced a can and a squeeze-bulb siphon from the back of the van. The plan was to get gas from Ragland as well as borrowing his battery.

Quietly they walked down the alley to Ragland's truck. Tonel popped the hood and set to work extracting the battery while Jack began pumping gas from Ragland's tank. It felt stupid to be making such a complicated thing out of getting a car. Gretchen needed his help. Shouldn't he just walk around the corner and take his Mom's car?

Right about then Ragland appeared, gliding out of his backyard like a ghost, the barrel of his shotgun glinting in the streetlight. He was holding it level at his waist, pointing right at Jack's stomach.

"You hookworm," said Ragland. "I oughtta blow a hole in you."

Tonel jumped backward, letting the hood slam shut. "We just tryin' to use Daddy's van," he said. "We figured we could borrow your—"

"I'm gonna call the po-lice," said Ragland. "A night in jail be good for you two whelps."

"Oh yeah?" said Tonel. "How 'bout if I tell them what you do to them old men in the locker room? We saw you rollin' 'em up. Cops might even call it murder."

"You was in the lockers?" said Ragland, letting his gun droop.

"We undid the bolt, then came in through the grate in the ceiling," said Jack. "And then we let ourselves out. We didn't bother closing the bolt."

"Oh Lord," said Ragland after a pause. "You gotta help me now. Jump in my truck."

"How long have the mibracc been like that?" Jack asked Ragland as he drove them towards the club.

"Goin' on two weeks," said Ragland. "Right when they got them big glass jars. Was Mr. Gupta showed me about the stomach plugs. He got it from somethin' he seen on TV. The men like me to do 'em that way. I drain 'em every night, and plump 'em up in the mawnin'. We use the steam room. They been payin' me extra and, yeah Tonel, they even doin' some yard work for me."

"But what do it mean?" asked Tonel.

"That's a conundrum," said Ragland. "But I don't want to see what happens if they get out on their own."

As soon as he'd parked, Ragland was out the door and across the parking lot, still carrying his shotgun. Jack noticed that he'd left the keys in the ignition. Should he just take off and save Gretchen? But then Ragland glared back at them and gestured with his gun. Jack had a feeling the old man wouldn't hesitate to use it. Somewhat unwillingly, Jack and Tonel went to lend him their support.

From the terrace, Jack could see past the barbeque wagon and into the air-conditioned grill where Les Trucklee was pouring out brandy for a last few red-faced Killeville gentry. He could hear their voices braying even through the closed windows. Nasal, buzzing, self-satisfied. Tomorrow Jack would be gone—if only he could make it through tonight.

The locker room door was still unbolted, and knob was unlocked. Ragland led the boys right in. The air was thick with vapor; voices boomed from the steam room. It was the mibracc, sounding hale and well rested.

Holding his shotgun at the ready, Ragland peered into the sauna. Two of the skins were still on the floor where they'd slithered; the other three had already plumped up. They were talking about golf, poker, and politics in that bone-dull Killeville way that made it impossible to hear more than a few consecutive phrases.

"Get back in your bags!" Ragland told them. "It's still night."

Mr. Cuthbert looked over and gave Ragland the finger, baring his top row of ivory yellow teeth. And then Mr. Atlee strode over and grabbed the barrel of Ragland's gun.

The blast of the shotgun shell was shockingly loud in the small, tiled space. Jack's ears rang, he felt like he might be permanently deafened.

Though a large piece of Mr. Atlee's stomach was gone, the mibracc was still standing. Worse than that, he'd taken control of the shotgun. Mr. Atlee struck Ragland on the side of the head with the gunstock, dropping him. And then he leveled the barrels at Jack and Tonel. The two took to their heels. There was a blast as they reached the door; it missed them, but the buckshot hailed against the lockers.

Without looking back for Ragland, or taking any time with the lock, they ran for their lives and jumped in the old man's truck. Tonel drove them down Egmont Avenue, tires squealing, the truck slewing from side to side. Slowly Jack's hearing returned. His phone had a message on it; he'd missed the ring. It was Gretchen.

"Where are you?" cried the voice, anxious and thin. "Dad's already driving Albert and me to the Casa Linda! Oh, Jack, please help me now and I'll always—" Abruptly the message broke off. All thoughts of calling the police or going back to try and save Ragland flew from Jack's mind.

He and Tonel made their way through downtown Killeville and out Route 501. The flare of neon lit up the muggy, moonless August sky. Here was the Banana Split, with Danny's heavy Pig Chef Harley parked in front among the SUVs and pickups. Next door was Rash Decisions Tattoo. And beyond that was the dirty pink concrete bulk of Casa Linda, faint slits of light showing through some of the tightly drawn blinds.

Gretchen was on them as soon as they got out of the car, running over from the shadows of the Casa Linda parking lot.

"Jack! You've come to save me!"

"Where's Chesney?"

"Oh, he went inside alone," said Gretchen airily. "I put down my foot. I'm still available, Jack." She took hold of his arm and pointed toward Rash Decisions Tattoo. "Justice of the Peace Ronnie Blevins is right in there."

Jack felt like his head was exploding. "Damn it, Gretchen, it's too much. You can't keep scamming me like this."

"Oh, I'll settle for one last hole six blowout," said Gretchen. "Get Danny to buy us some beer. I see his bike over there."

"We stayin' away from Danny tonight," said Tonel. "He way too spun. I can buy us beer. What about that Pinka Wright, Gretchen? Did you talk to her or not?"

"I can call her now," said Gretchen. "We'll drive by her house on the way to the club. I bet she'll come out with you. She craves the wild side."

"Was it all a lie about Albert Chesney?" demanded Jack.

"Albert really does say the last battle is tomorrow," said Gretchen. "At the tabernacle he was showing this video of donut-shaped flying saucers. Supposedly they're going to come for us at dawn, full of devils. But angels will be here to help fight them. Albert says if six righteous people step forward they can save the day. But I think we ought to leave before he comes back out of the motel. He's real intent on that girding his loins thing." Seeing Jack's face, Gretchen burst into laughter. "Why are you always so uptight?"

So they bounced out of there without seeing Chesney. Tonel got beer from a downtown 7-11 clerked by his cousin. Some of the people at the store recognized Ragland's truck, which reminded Jack that, oh God, they'd left Ragland lying on the steam room floor at the mercy of the mibracc. What with the pot gum and the worry about Gretchen he'd completely spaced that out. It was a good thing they were heading back to the club.

Meanwhile Gretchen worked her phone and not only did they pick up Pinka, but a bunch more people said they'd meet them at the parking lot—arty Tyler Simpson, pretty Geli Yoder, Lulu Anders the Goth, fat Louie Levy, and even goody-goody Lucy Candler and her jock boyfriend Rick Stazanik.

The Killeville Country Club was dark, save for Les Trucklee's office on the second floor of the club's front side. Maybe he was waiting up for Danny Dank. But Les wouldn't be a problem for the kids. He turned a blind eye to their hole six parties.

Some of the kids were already there, waiting and drinking beer.

"Come help me see about Ragland," said Jack to Gretchen and Tonel.

"Yuck," said Gretchen. "In the men's locker room?"

"Chill," said Tonel, who was in a heavy conversation with Pinka. "I'm gettin' over."

"Let's party," said Rick Stazanik. This was the first hole six event he and Lucy had attended, and they were gung-ho to get it on.

"There might be some zombies out there," warned Jack. "The mibracc. You guys have to help me check if they left a corpse in the locker room."

"How spine-tingling," said Lulu.

"Safety in numbers," said Louie Levy. "We'll stick together."

So before heading out onto the links, the gang did a quick check in the locker room for Ragland. No sign of him. And when Jack used Ragland's master-thumbs to try and show them golf bags of bourbon, the bags turned up as empty as the gas tank on Vincente's van.

They had some fun grab-assing and scaring each other on the long trek out to the green of hole six. But in truth there was no sign of anything out of the ordinary. There were not a few laughs at Jack's expense. And then they settled down on their green, drinking beer and chewing marijuana gum. Tyler Simpson had brought speakers and a music player with all the alternative hits of their high-school years.

After a bit Jack and Gretchen crept off to a private spot twenty meters past the green and made love. It was, after all, their last night together. As always, Jack used a condom. He'd been a dope to let her scare him with that pregnancy thing.

"Will you remember me at college?" Gretchen asked Jack. Her face looked big and open under his. She dropped most of her games when they were alone like this.

"I will. It's not all that far. You can come visit. Or I'll visit here. You'll have your classes too." Gretchen was going to be studying at a local business college.

In the distance Jack heard the roar of a motorcycle pulling into the lot. Danny. He kind of hoped Danny was here to see Les and not here for the hole six party. What a weird day this had been. He was still uneasily wondering where Ragland and the mibracc had gone. After a bit, he and Gretchen went back with the others on the green.

An hour later, in between the songs, Jack began hearing the mibracc's voices, accompanied by the clink of tools in dirt. He tried to tell the others, but they either couldn't hear it or they weren't interested, not even Tonel or Gretchen. It sounded to Jack as if the mibracc were somewhere close to the clubhouse. That meant that, all in all, it would be safer to stay out here till dawn. Lots of people would be showing up for the Killeville Barbeque Breakfast Golf Classic. And then Jack could get his suitcase, say good-bye to Mom, and hop the 8:37 a.m. bus to college. He wished he'd called Mom. She'd be worrying about him.

About four in the morning, Lulu Anders, Louie Levy, Lucy Candler, and Rick Stazanik wanted to leave. By now Jack had gotten them to notice the mibracc's voices, but the four figured that if they went all together there wouldn't be a problem. Jack warned them not to, getting pretty passionate about it. But they wouldn't listen. They thought he was spun. They were more scared of their parents than of the mibracc.

Their screams across the golf course were terrible to hear. Four sets of screams, then nothing but the muttering of the mibracc and the scraping of metal against soil.

When dawn broke, the remaining six kids were flaked out around a mound of empty beer cans. Geli and Tonel were asleep. Pinka had chewed a lot of marijuana gum and was jabbering to Tyler, who was delicately jabbing at his music machine's controls, mixing the sounds in with Pinka's words. Gretchen and Jack were just sitting there staring toward the clubhouse, fearful of what they'd see.

As the mist cleared, they were able to pick out the figures of the five mibracc, busy at the eighteenth green, right by the terrace. They had shovels; they'd carved the green down into a cupped depression. Like a satellite dish. The surface of the dish gleamed, something slick was all over it—smeel. There was a slim projecting twist of smeel at the dish's center. The green had become an antenna beaming signals into who knew what unknown dimensions.

On the terrace the large barbeque grill was already fired up, greasy smoke pouring from its little tin chimney. Next to it was a sturdy table piled with bloody meat. And standing there working the grill was—Danny.

"Let's go," said Jack. "I have to get out of this town."

He shook Tonel and Geli awake. There was a moth resting on Tonel's cheek, another moth with a human head. Before flapping off, it smiled at Jack and said something in an encouraging tone—though it was too faint to understand.

"I been dreaming about heaven," said Tonel, rubbing his hands against his eyes. "What up, dog?"

Jack pointed toward the clubhouse and now all the kids saw what Danny was doing.

Geli, Pinka, and Tyler decided to stay out at hole six, but Jack, Gretchen, and Tonel worked their way closer to the clubhouse, taking cover in the patches of rough. Maybe they could still fix things. And Jack couldn't get it out of his mind that he still might catch his bus.

He was seeing more and more of the moths with human heads. Their wings shed the brown-gray moth dust and turned white in the rays of the rising sun. They were little angels.

A cracked trumpet note sounded from the heavens, then another and another. "Look," said Gretchen pointing up. "It's all true."

"God help us," said Tonel, gazing at the gathering UFOs.

A silver torus landed by the clubhouse, homing right in on the eighteenth green. Some creatures got out, things more or less like large praying mantises—with long, jointed legs, curving abdomens, bulging compound eyes, and mouths that were cruel triangular beaks. A dozen of them. They headed straight for the barbeque wagon.

Stacked on the table beside the barbeque wagon were the headless butchered corpses of Lulu Anders, Louie Levy, Lucy Candler, and Rick Stazanik, ready to be cooked. The aliens—or devils—crossed the terrace, their large bodies rocking from side to side, their green abdomens wobbling. Danny swung up the barbeque wagon's curved door. There in the double-hog barbeque grill were the bodies of Les and Ragland, already well crisped.

Sweating and grinning, Danny wielded a cleaver and a three-tined fork, cutting loose some tender barbeque for the giant mantises. The monsters bit into the meat, their jaws snipping out neat triangles.

Danny's eyes were damned, tormented, mad. He was wearing something strange on his head, not a chef's hat, no, it was floppy and bloody and hairy and with big ears—it was poor Les Trucklee's scalp. Danny was a Pig Chef.

Over by the parking lot, early-bird golfers and barbeque breakfasters were starting to arrive. One by one the mibracc beat them to death with golf clubs and dragged them to the barbeque wagon's side. Even with the oily smoke and the smell of fresh blood in the air, none of the new arrivals thought to worry when the five familiar men from the back room approached them.

"The end of the world," breathed Gretchen.

"I have to see Mom," said Jack brokenly. "Get my suitcase and see Mom. I have to leave today."

"I want to get Daddy," said Tonel.

The three looped around the far side of the clubhouse and managed to hail down a pickup truck with a lawnmower in back. The driver was old Luke Taylor.

"Can you carry us home?" asked Tonel.

"I can," said Luke, dignified and calm. "What up at the country club?"

"There's a flying saucer with devils eating people!" said Gretchen. "It's the end!"

Luke glanced over at her, not believing what he heard. "Maybe," he said equably, "But I'm still gonna cut Mrs. Bowen's grass befo' the sun gets too hot."

Luke dropped them at Vaughan Electronics. Jack and Gretchen ran around the corner to the rectory. The house was quiet, with the faint chatter of children's voices from the back yard. Odd for a Sunday morning. Rev. Langhorne should be bustling around getting ready for church. Jack used his key to open the door, making as little noise as possible. Gretchen was right at his side.

It was Gretchen who noticed the spot on the banister. A dried bloody print from a very small hand. Out in the backyard the children were singing. They were busy with something; Jack heard a clank and a rattle. He didn't dare go back there to see.

Moving fast, Jack and Gretchen tiptoed upstairs. There was blood on the walls near the Langhorne parents' room. Jack went straight for his mother's single bedroom, blessedly unspotted with blood. But the room was empty.

"Mom?" whispered Jack.

There was a slight noise from the closet.

Jack swung open the closet door. No sign of his mother—but, wait, there was a big lump on the top shelf, covered over with a silk scarf.

"Is that you, Mom?" said Jack, scared what he might find.

The paisley scarf slid down. Jack's mother was curled

up on the shelf in her nightgown, her eyes wide and staring.

"Those horrible children," she said in a tiny, strained voice. "They butchered their parents in bed. I hid."

"Hurry, Mrs. Vaughan," said Gretchen. She was standing against the wall, peeking out the back window. "They're starting up the grill."

And, yes, Jack could smell the lighter fluid and the smoke. Four little Pig Chefs in the making. A smallish alien craft slid past the window, wedging itself down into the backyard.

Somewhat obsessively, Jack went into his bedroom and fetched his packed suitcase before leading Gretchen and his Mom to the front door. It just about cost them too much time. For as the three of them crept down the front porch steps they heard the slamming of the house's back door and the drumming of little footsteps.

Faster than it takes to tell it, Jack, Gretchen, and Jessie Vaughan were in Jessie's car, Jack at the wheel, slewing around the corner. They slowed only to pick up Tonel and Vincente, and then they were barreling out of town on Route 501.

"Albert was saying we should come to the Casa Linda and help him," said Gretchen. "He said he'd be watching from the roof. He said he needed five pure hearts to pray with him. Six of us in all. We're pure, aren't we?"

Jack might not have stopped, but as it happened, there was a roadblock in the highway right by the Casa Linda. The police all had pointed ears. The coffee in their cups was continually swirling. And the barbeque pit beside the Banana Split was fired up. A gold UFO was just now angling down for a landing.

"I'm purely ready to pray my ass off," said Vincente.

When they jumped out of the car, the police tried to take hold of the five, to hustle them toward the barbeque. But a sudden flight of the little angels distracted the pig-eared cops. The tiny winged beings beat at the men's cruel faces, giving the five pure hearts a chance.

Clutching his suitcase like a talisman, Jack led Gretchen, Jessie, Tonel, and Vincente across the parking lot to the Casa Linda. They pounded up the motel's outdoor concrete stairs, all the way to the roof. The pointy-eared police were too busy with the next carload of victims to chase after them. Over by the Banana Split, hungry mantises were debarking from the gold donut.

They found Albert Chesney at the low parapet of the motel roof, staring out across the rolling hills of Killeville. He had a calm, satisfied expression. His prophecies were coming true.

"Behold the city of sin," he said, gesturing toward Killeville's pitifully sparse town center, its half dozen worn old office buildings. "See how the mighty have been brought low."

"How do we make it stop, Albert?" asked Gretchen.

"Let us join hands and pray," said Chesney.

So they stood there, the early morning breeze playing upon the six of them—Albert, Gretchen, Jack, Jessie, Tonel, and Vincente. There were maybe three dozen toroidal UFOs scattered around Killeville by now. And beside each of them was a plume of greasy smoke.

Jack hadn't prayed in quite some time. As boarders in the rectory, they'd had to go to Reverend Langhorne's church every Sunday, but the activity had struck him as exclusively social, with no connection to any of the deep philosophical and religious questions he might chew over with friends, like, "Where did all this come from?" or, "What happens after I die?"

But now, oh yes, he was praying. And it's safe to say the five others were praying too. Something like, "Save us, save the earth, make the aliens go away, dear God please help."

As they prayed, the mothlike angels got bigger. The prayers were pumping energy into the good side of the Shekinah Glory. Before long the angels were the size of people. They were more numerous than Jack had initially realized.

"Halle-friggin-lujah!" said Vincente, and they prayed some more.

The angels grew to the size of cars, to the size of buildings. The Satanic flying donuts sprang into the air and fired energy bolts at them. The angels grew yet taller, as high as the sky. Their faces were clear, solemn, terrible to behold. The evil UFOs were helpless against them, puny as gnats. Peeking through his fingers, Jack saw one of the alien craft go flying across the horizon toward an angel, and saw the impact as the great holy being struck with a hand the size of a farm. The shattered bits of the UFO shrank into nothingness, as if melting in the sun. It was only a matter of minutes until the battle was done. The closest angel fixed Jack with an unbearable gaze, then made a gesture that might have been a benediction. And now the great beings rotated in some unseen direction and angled out of view.

"Praise God!" said Albert Chesney when it was done.

"Praise God," echoed Jack. "But that's enough for now, Lord. Don't have the whole Last Judgment today. Let me go to college first. Give us at least six more years."

And it was so.

A Greyhound bus drew even with the Casa Linda and pulled over for a stop. BLACKSBURG, read the sign above the bus window. Jack bid the quickest of farewells to his mother and his friends, and then, whooping and yelling, he ran down the stairs with his suitcase and hopped aboard.

The Killeville Barbeque Massacre trials dragged on through the fall. Jack and Albert had to testify a few times. Most of the Pig Chef defendants got off with temporary insanity pleas, basing their defense on smeel-poisoning, although no remaining samples of smeel could be found. The police officers were of course pardoned, and Danny Dank got the death penalty. The cases of Banks, Price, Sydnor, and Rainey were moot—for with their appetites whetted by the flesh of the children's parents, the mantises had gone ahead and eaten the four fledgling Pig Chefs.

The trials didn't draw as much publicity as one might have expected. The crimes were simply too disgusting. And the Killeville citizenry had collective amnesia regarding the UFOs. Some of the Day Six Synodites remembered, but the Synod was soon split into squabbling subsects by a series of schisms. With his onerous parole conditions removed in return for his help with the trials, Albert Chesney left town for California to become a computer game developer.

Jessie Vaughan got herself ordained as a deacon and took over the pastoral duties at St. Anselm's church. At Christmas Jessie celebrated the marriage of Jack to Gretchen Karst—who was indeed pregnant. Tonel took leave from the Navy to serve as best man.

Gretchen transferred into Virginia Polytechnic with Jack for the spring term. The couple did well in their studies. Jack majored in Fluid Engineering and Gretchen in Computer Science. And after graduation they somehow ended up moving into the rectory with Jessie and opening a consulting firm in Killeville.

As for the men in the back room of the country club—they completely dropped out of sight. The prudent reader would be well advised to keep an eye out for mibracc in his or her hometown. And pay close attention to the fluid dynamics of coffee, juice, and alcoholic beverages. Any undue rotation could be a sign of smeel.

The end is near.

NOTES

For the years 1980–1986, I lived with my wife and kids in Lynchburg, Virginia, the home of televangelist Jerry Falwell and headquarters of his right-wing Moral Majority political action group. I ended up writing a number of stories about Lynchburg, transreally dubbing it Killeville.

During our final years in Lynchburg, I was proud to be a member of the Oakwood Country Club—it was a pleasant place and the dues were modest enough that even an unemployed cyberpunk writer could afford them. I was always intrigued by a group of men who sat drinking bourbon and playing cards in a small windowless room off the men's locker room—isolated from the civilizing force of the fair sex. Somehow I formulated the idea that at night the men were rolled up like apricot leather and stored in glass carboys of whiskey that sat within their golf bags.

I was thinking of a power-chord story somewhat analogous to Phil Dick's "The Father Thing." The power chord here is "alien-controlled pod people." Another archetype I wanted to touch upon is the Pig Chef, an icon that's always disturbed me. I wanted to push this concept to its logical conclusion, so that everyone would finally understand the Pig Chef's truly evil nature! Yet another aspect of my story is that I wanted to use the format of the classic last-night-of-high-school epic, *American Graffiti*.

Despite all my pontificating about the virtues of logic in my interview with Terry Bisson in these pages, "The Men in the Back Room at the Country Club" is pretty much at the surreal end of the spectrum, as is often the case with horror-tinged tales. Naturally I had trouble getting anyone to publish it. Fortunately, the writer and editor Eileen Gunn gets my sense of humor. Like my earlier story "Jenna and Me," this weird tale found a home in Eileen's online magazine *Infinite Matrix* at www.infinitematrix.net, which was, as long as it lasted, something like a clear channel border-radio station.

SURFING THE GNARL

WHAT IS GNARL?

I USE *gnarl* IN AN IDIOSYNCRATIC and somewhat technical sense; I use it to mean a level of complexity that lies in the zone between predictability and randomness.

The original meaning of "gnarl" was simply "a knot in the wood of a tree." In California surfer slang, "gnarly" came to describe complicated, rapidly changing surf conditions. And then, by extension, something gnarly came to be anything with surprisingly intricate detail. As a late-arriving and perhaps over-assimilated Californian, I get a kick out of the word.

Do note that "gnarly" can also mean "disgusting." Soon after I moved to California in 1986, I was at an art festival where a caterer was roasting a huge whole pig on a spit above a gas-fired grill the size of a car. Two teenage boys walked by and looked silently at the pig. Finally one of them observed, "Gnarly, dude." In the same vein, my son has been heard to say, "Never ever eat anything gnarly." And having your body become old and gnarled isn't necessarily a pleasant thing. But here I only want to talk about gnarl in a good kind of way.

Clouds, fire, and water are gnarly in the sense of being beautifully intricate, with purposeful-looking but not quite comprehensible patterns. And of course all living things are gnarly, in that they inevitably do things that are much more complex than one might have expected. As I mentioned, the shapes of tree branches are the standard example of gnarl. The life cycle of a jellyfish is way gnarly. The wild three-dimensional paths that a hummingbird sweeps out are kind of gnarly too, and, if the truth be told, your ears are gnarly as well.

I'm a writer first and foremost, but for much of my life I had a day-job as a professor, first in mathematics and then in computer science. Although I'm back to being a freelance writer now, I spent twenty years in the dark Satanic mills of Silicon Valley. Originally I thought I was going there as a kind of literary lark like an overbold William Blake manning a loom in Manchester. But eventually I went native on the story. It changed the way I think. I drank the Kool-Aid.

I derived my notion of gnarl from the work of the computer scientist Stephen Wolfram. I first met him in 1984, interviewing him for a science article I was writing. He made a big impression on me, and introduced me to the dynamic graphical computations known as cellular automata, or CAs for short. The so-called Game of Life is the best-known CA. You start with a few lit-up pixels on a computer screen. Each pixel "looks" at the eight nearest pixels, counts how many are "on" and adjusts its state according to this total, using a fixed rule. All of the pixels do this at once, so the screen behaves like a parallel computation. The patterns of dots grow, reproduce, and/or die, sometimes generating persistent moving patterns known as gliders. I became fascinated by CAs, and it's thanks in part to Wolfram that I switched from teaching math to teaching computer science.

Wolfram summarized his ideas in his thick 2002 tome, *A New Kind of Science*. To me, having known Wolfram for many years by then, the ideas in the book seemed obviously true. I went on to write my own nonfiction book, *The Lifebox, the Seashell, and the Soul*, partly to popularize Wolfram's ideas, and partly to expatiate upon my own notions of the meaning of computation. A work of early geek philosophy. Most scientists found the new ideas to be—as Wolfram sarcastically put it—either trivial or wrong. When a set of ideas provokes such resistance, it's a sign of an impending paradigm shift.

o o o

So what does Wolfram say? I'll break this into four points.

(1) Wolfram starts by arguing that we can think of any natural process as a computation, that is, you can see anything as a deterministic procedure that works out the consequences of some initial conditions. Instead of viewing the world as made of atoms or of curved space or of natural laws, we can try viewing it as made of computations. Keep in mind that a "computer" doesn't have to be made of wires and silicon chips in a box. It can be any real-world phenomenon you like.

(2) Having studied a very large number of visually interesting computations called cellular automata, Wolfram concluded that there are basically three kinds of computations and three corresponding kinds of natural processes.

Predictable. Processes that are ultimately without surprise. This may be because they eventually die out and become constant, or because they're repetitive. Think of a checkerboard, or a clock, or a fire that burns down to dead ashes.

Gnarly. Processes that are structured in interesting ways but are nonetheless unpredictable. Here we think of a vine, or a waterfall, or the startling yet computable digits of pi.

Random. Processes that are completely messy and unstructured. Think of the molecules eternally bouncing off each other in air, or the cosmic rays from outer space.

The gnarly middle zone is where it's at. Essentially all of the interesting patterns in physics and biology are gnarly. Gnarly processes hold out the lure of being partially understandable, but they resist falling into dull predictability.

(3) Wolfram's third tenet is that all gnarly computations are in fact universal computations. "Universal computation" is used in the technical computer-scientific sense of a computation that can in fact emulate any other computation. Universal computations aren't at all rare. Every desktop or smartphone computer is a universal computer in the sense that it can, given enough time and memory, model the behavior of any other such computer.

Given that physical processes are a type of computation, it's natural that the virtual worlds of our videogames support a kind of artificial physics. The objects in these little worlds bounce off each other, the projectiles follow trajectories shaped by "gravity," the race-cars skid and spin out when they make overly sharp turns.

Wolfram says we can turn things around. An interesting physical process is a gnarly computation, any gnarly computation is a universal computation, therefore any interesting real world process can, in principle, emulate any other naturally occurring process.

In some sense we're all the same: a cloud can emulate an oak tree, a flickering flame can model a human mind, a dripping faucet can behave like the stock market.

If this strikes you as a strange way to think, you're in good company. The universality of naturally occurring gnarly computations is something that the older generation of scientists finds baffling and outrageous.

(4) Nothing of any significance in the natural world is predictable. Science's dreams of ultimate mastery are self-aggrandizing horseshit.

How so? As argued in point (3), all the interesting naturally occurring computations are gnarly computations, and these gnarly computations are universal computations with the ability of emulating each other. Given these facts, it's possible, via some ironclad computer-science legerdemain, to prove that the interesting processes of nature are inherently unpredictable. The problem is that if you can predict the behavior of a particular universal computation, you run head-on into the Unsolvability of the Halting Problem, a paradoxical result proved by the early computer scientist Alan Turing in 1936.

What, by the way, do I mean by "predicting a process"? This means to have some procedure for determining the processes result very much faster than the time it takes to simply let the process run. The point of result (4) is that there are no quick short-cut methods for finding out what a gnarly computation will do. The only way to really find out what the weather is going to be like tomorrow is to wait twenty-four hours and see. The only way for me to find out what I'm going to put into the final paragraph of a book is to finish writing the book.

It's worth repeating this point. We will never find any magical tiny theory that allows us to make quick pencil-and-paper calculations about the future. Sometimes scientists—or science-fiction writers—have speculated that there's some compact master-formula capable of predicting the future with a few strokes of a pencil. And many still have an internal faith in some slightly more sophisticated restatement of this.

But, as Wolfram so convincingly argues, the world, being gnarly, is inherently unpredictable. We have no hope of control. On the plus side, gnarl is a bit better behaved than the random. We can hope to ride the waves.

o o o

Anything involving fluids can be a rich source of gnarl—even a cup of tea. The most orderly state of a liquid is, of course, for it to be standing still. If one lets water run rather slowly down a channel, the water moves smoothly, with a predictable pattern of ripples.

As more water is put into a channel, the ripples begin to crisscross and waver. Eddies and whirlpools appear—and with turbulent flow we have the birth of gnarl.

Once a massive amount of water is poured down the channel, we get a less interesting random state in which the water is seething. At this point I should caution that I'm using "random" the loose sense of "having no perceivable pattern." It might be that a liquid or some other complex process is in fact obeying a deterministic rule and is what we more properly call "pseudorandom." But I'll just say "random" to keep the discussion simple.

Besides the flow of water, another good day-to-day example of a gnarly physical process is a tree whose leaves and branches are trembling in the breeze. Here's some journal notes I wrote about a tree I saw while backpacking near Big Sur with my daughter Isabel and her husband Gus in May 2003.

> Green hills, wonderfully curved, the gnarly oaks, fractal white cloud puffs, the Pacific Ocean hanging anomalously high in the sky, fog-quilted.
>
> I got up first, right before sunrise, and I was looking at a medium-sized pine tree just down the ridge from my tent. Gentle dawn breezes were playing over the tree, and every single one of its needles was quivering, oscillating through its own characteristic range of frequencies, and the needle clumps and branches were rocking as well, working their way around their own particular phase space, the whole motion harmonious in the extreme. Insects buzzed about the tree, and, having looked in the microscope so much of late, I could easily visualize the microorganisms upon the needles, in the beads of sap, beneath the bark, in the insects' guts—the tree a microcosmos. The sun came rolling up over the ridge, gilding my pine. With all its needles aflutter it was like an anemone, like a dancer, like a cartoon character with a halo of alertness rays.
>
> "I love you," I said to the tree, for just that moment not even needing to reach past the tree to imagine any divinity behind it, for just that moment seeing the tree itself as a god.
>
> When we got home there were my usual daily problems to confront and I felt uptight. And now, writing these notes, I ask how can I get some serenity?

I have the laptop here on a cafe table under a spring-green tree in sunny blue-sky Los Gatos. I look up at the tree overhead, a linden with very small pale fresh green leaves. And yes the leaves are doing the hand jive. The branches rocking. The very image of my wandering thoughts, eternally revisiting the same topics. It's good.

The trees, the leaves, the clouds, my mind, it's all the same, all so beautifully gnarly.

GNARL AND LITERATURE

As a reader, I've always sought the gnarl, that is, I like to find odd, interesting, unpredictable kinds of books, possibly with outré or transgressive themes. My favorites would include Jack Kerouac and William Burroughs, Robert Sheckley and Phil Dick, Jorge Luis Borges and Thomas Pynchon.

Once again, a gnarly process is complex and unpredictable without being random. If a story hews to some very familiar pattern, it feels stale. But if absolutely anything can happen, a story becomes as unengaging as someone else's dream. The gnarly zone lies at the interface between logic and fantasy.

William Burroughs was an ascended master of the gnarl. He believed in having his work take on an autonomous life to the point of becoming a world that the author inhabits. "The writer has been there or he can't write about it. . . . [Writers] are trying to create a universe in which they have lived or where they would like to live. To write it, they must go there and submit to conditions that they might not have bargained for." (From "Remembering Jack

Kerouac" in *The Adding Machine: Selected Essays*, Seaver Books, 1986.)

In order to present some ideas about how gnarl applies to literature in general, and to science-fiction in particular, the table below summarizes how gnarliness makes its way into literature in four areas: subject matter, plot, scientific speculation, and social commentary.

In drawing up the table, I found it useful to distinguish between *low gnarl* and *high gnarl*. Low gnarl is close to being periodic and predictable, while high gnarl is closer to being fully random.

Keep in mind that I'm not saying any particular row of the table is absolutely better than the others. My purpose here is taxonomic rather than prescriptive. To this end, rather than using the word "predictable" and "random" to refer to the lowest and highest levels of complexity, I'll use the less judgmental words "classic" and "surreal."

In order to spark discussion, I've positioned the names of some of my favorite fantasy or science-fiction authors in the first cells of each row. Note that some authors may write novels in various modes—Terry Bisson's *Pirates of the Universe*, for instance, is high gnarl and transreal, while his *The Pickup Artist* is a surreal shaggy-dog story. Also note that any given novel may have different complexity levels relative to the four columns.

In any case, if you disagree with my classifications, so much the better—my main goal is to offer a tool for thought. In the four sections to come, I'll say a bit about the thinking that went into my table's four right-hand columns.

TABLE: GNARL IN LITERATURE

COMPLEXITY LEVEL. SAMPLE AUTHORS.	SUBJECT MATTER	PLOT	SCIENTIFIC SPECULATION	COMMENTARY
Classic. J.R.R. Tolkien, Isaac Asimov, Kage Baker.	Genre literature modeled on existing books or folktales.	A plot that hews to a standard formula.	Rote magic or pedagogic science, emphasizing limits rather than possibilities.	Unthinking advocacy of the status quo.
Low gnarl. Robert Heinlein, William Gibson, Bruce Sterling, Cory Doctorow, Karen Joy Fowler.	Realism, modeled on the actual world or a closely imagined fictional world.	A plot structure embodying a real-world flow of events. "Life is stranger than fiction."	Moderate thought experiments: the consequences of a few plausible new ideas.	Comedy: Noticing that existing social trends lead to absurdities.
High gnarl. Charles Stross, Robert Sheckley, Phillip K. Dick, Eileen Gunn.	Transrealism, in which the author's personal experience is enhanced by transcendent elements.	A plot obtained by starting with a real-life story and enhancing it, as in a fairy tale.	Extreme thought experiments: the consequences of some completely unexpected new ideas.	Satire: Extrapolating social trends into mad yet logical environments.
Surreal. Douglas Adams, John Shirley, Terry Bisson.	Fabulation, fantasy, or science fiction of unreal worlds.	Like a shaggy-dog story, possibly based on dreams or collage-like juxtapositions.	Irrational and inconsistent; anything goes. Logic is abandoned.	Jape, parody, anarchist humor.

SUBJECT MATTER AND TRANSREALISM

Regarding the kinds of characters and situations that one can write about, my sense is that we have a four-fold spectrum of possible modes: simple genre writing with stock characters, mimetic realism, the heightened kind of realism that I call transrealism, and full-on fabulation. Both realism and transrealism lie in the gnarly zone. Speaking specifically in terms of subject matter, I'd be inclined to say that transrealism is gnarlier, as it allows for more possibilities.

What do I mean by transrealism? Early in my writing career, my friend Gregory Gibson advised, "It would be great to write science fiction and have it be about your everyday life." I took that to heart. The science fiction novels of Philip K. Dick were an inspiration on this front as well.

In 1983, having read a remark where the writer Norman Spinrad referred to Dick's novel *A Scanner Darkly* as "transcendental autobiography, " I came up with the term *transrealism*, to represent a synthesis between fantastic fabulation (trans) and closely observed character-driven fiction (realism), and I began advocating a transrealist method of writing.

- *Trans*. Use the SF and fantasy tropes to express deep psychic archetypes. Put in science-fictional events or technologies which reflect deeper aspects of people and society. Manipulate subtext.
- *Realism*. Possibly include a main character similar to yourself and, in any case, base your characters on real people you know, or on combinations of them.

Twenty novels later, I no longer feel I have to go whole hog with transrealism and cast my friends and family into my books. I think they got a little tired of it. For awhile there, I was like Ingmar Bergman, continually making movies with the same little troupe of actors/family/friends. These days I'm more likely to collage together a variety of observed traits to make my characters, like a magpie gathering up bright scraps for a nest.

I've come to think that you can in fact write transreally without overtly using your own life or specific people that you know. Even without having any characters who are particularly like myself, I can write closely observed works about my own life experiences. And if I'm transmuting these experiences with the alchemy of science fiction, the result is transreal. So I might restate the principles of transrealism like this.

- *Trans.* The author raises the action to a higher level by infusing magic or weird science, choosing tropes so as to intensify and augment some artistically chosen aspects of reality. Trans might variously stand for transfigurative, transformative, transcendental, transgressive, or transsexual.
- *Realism.* The author uses real-world ideas, emotions, perceptions that he or she has personally experienced or witnessed.

PLOT AND EMERGENCE

In the table's next column, I present a fourfold range of plot structures. At the low end of complexity, we have standardized plots, at the high end, we have no large-scale plot at all, and in between we have the gnarly somewhat unpredictable plots. These can be found in two kinds of ways, either by mimicking reality precisely, or by amplifying reality with incursions of psychically meaningful events.

A characteristic feature of any complex process is that you can't look at what's going on today and immediately deduce what will be happening in a few weeks. It's necessary to have the world run step-by-step through the intervening ticks of time. Gnarly computations are unpredictable; they don't allow for short-cuts. Thus, as I mentioned before, the last chapter of a novel with a gnarly plot will be, even in principle, unpredictable from the contents of the first chapter.

Although I believe this, over the years I've come to feel that it's not a bad idea to maintain an outline, however inaccurate. The detailed eddies of the story's flow will indeed have to work themselves out during the writing, but there's no harm in having some sluices and gutters to guide the narrative process along a harmonious and satisfying course.

I've learned that if I start writing a novel with no plot outline at all, two things happen. First of all, the readers can tell. Some will be charmed by the spontaneity, but some will complain that the book feels improvised, like a shaggy-dog story. Second, if I'm working without a plot outline, I'm going to experience some really painful and anxious days when everything seems broken, and I have no idea how to proceed. My mentor Robert Sheckley referred to these periods in the compositional process as "black points."

These days, writing an outline makes writing a novel easier on me. Perhaps it's a matter of mature craftsmanship versus youthful passion. Or maybe I'm just getting old. I've developed a fairly elaborate process. Even before I start writing a new book, I create an accompanying notes document in which I accumulate outlines, scene sketches and the like. The notes documents end up being very nearly as long as my books, and when the book comes out, I usually post the corresponding notes document online for perusal by those few who are very particularly interested in that book or in my working methods. (Links to these notes documents and some of my essays on writing can be found at www.rudyrucker.com/writing.)

It goes almost without saying that my outlines change as I work. Things emerge. It's like life! After writing any scene in a given chapter, I find that I have to go back and revise my prior outline of the following scenes.

In the end, only the novel itself is the perfect outline of the novel. Only the territory itself can be the perfect map. In this connection, I think of Jorge Luis Borges's one-paragraph fiction, "On Exactitude in Science," that contains this sentence: "In time, those Unconscionable Maps no longer satisfied, and the Cartographers' Guilds struck a Map of the Empire whose size was that of the Empire, and which coincided point for point with it." (*Collected Fictions*, 225).

Outline or not, the only way to discover the ending of a truly living book is to set yourself in motion and think constantly about the novel for months or years, writing all the while. The characters and gimmicks and social situations bounce off each other like eddies in a turbulent wakes, like gliders in a cellular automaton simulation, like vines twisting around each other in a jungle. And only time and extensive mental computation will tell you how the story ends. As I keep stressing, gnarly processes have no perfectly predictive short-cuts.

SCIENTIFIC SPECULATION AND THOUGHT EXPERIMENTS

What stampedes are to westerns or murders are to mysteries, *power chords* are to science fiction. I'm talking about certain classic tropes that have the visceral punch of heavy musical riffs: blaster guns, spaceships, time machines, aliens, telepathy, flying saucers, warped space, faster-than-light travel, immersive virtual reality, clones, robots, teleportation, alien-controlled pod people, endless shrinking, the shattering of planet Earth, intelligent goo, antigravity, starships, ecodisaster, pleasure-center zappers, alternate universes, nanomachines, mind viruses, higher dimensions, a cosmic computation that generates our reality, and, of course, the attack of the giant ants.

When a writer uses an SF power chord, there is an implicit understanding with the informed readers that this is indeed familiar ground. And it's expected the writer will do something fresh with the trope. "Make it new," as Ezra Pound said, several years before he went crazy.

Mainstream writers who dip a toe into what they daintily call "speculative fiction" tend not be aware of just how familiar are the chords they strum. And the mainstream critics are unlikely to call their cronies to task over failing to create original SF. They don't have a clue either. And we lowly science-fiction people are expected to be grateful when a mainstream writer stoops to filch a bespattered icon from our filthy wattle huts? Oh, wait, do I sound bitter?

When I use a power chord, I might place it into an unfamiliar context, perhaps describing it more intensely than usual, or perhaps using it for a novel thought experiment. I like it when my material takes on a life of its own. This leads to the gnarly zone. As with plot, it's a matter of working out unpredictable consequences of simple-seeming assumptions.

The reason why fictional thought experiments are so powerful is that, in practice, it's intractably difficult to visualize the side effects of new technological developments. Only if you place the new tech into a fleshed-out fictional world and simulate the effects on reality can you get a clear image of what might happen.

In order to tease out the subtler consequences of current trends, a complex fictional simulation is necessary; inspired narration is a more powerful tool than logical analysis. If I want to imagine, for instance, what our world would be like if ordinary objects like chairs or shoes were conscious, then the best way to make progress is to fictionally simulate a person discovering this.

The kinds of thought experiments I enjoy are different in intent and in execution from merely futurological investigations. My primary goal is not to make useful predictions that businessmen can use. I'm more interested in exploring the human condition, with literary power chord standing in for archetypal psychic forces.

Where to find material for our thought experiments? You don't have to be a scientist. As Kurt Vonnegut used to remark, most science fiction writers don't know much about science. But SF writers have an ability to pick out some odd new notion and set up a thought experiment. As Robert Sheckley remarked to me when he was living in a camper in my driveway, "At the heart of it all is a rage to extrapolate. Excuse me, shall I extrapolate that for you? Won't take a jiffy."

The most entertaining fantasy and SF writers have a rage to extrapolate; a zest for seeking the gnarl.

SOCIAL COMMENTARY AND SATIRE

I'm always uncomfortable when I'm described as a science-fiction humorist. I'm not trying to be funny in my work. It's just that things often happen to come out as amusing when I tell them the way I see them.

Wit involves describing the world as it actually is. And you experience a release of tension when the elephant in the living room is finally named. Wit is a critical-satirical process that can be more serious than the "humorous" label suggests.

The least-aware kinds of literature take society entirely at face value, numbly acquiescing in the myths and mores laid down by the powerful. These forms are dead, too cold.

At the other extreme, we have the chaotic forms of social commentary where everything under the sun becomes questionable and a subject for mockery. If everything's a joke, then nothing matters. This said, laughing like a crazy hyena can be fun.

In the gnarly zone, we have fiction that extrapolates social conventions to the point where the inherent contradictions become overt enough to provoke the shock of recognition and the concomitant release of laughter. At the low end of this gnarly zone we have observational commentary on the order of stand-up comedy. And at the higher end we get inspired satire.

In this vein, Sheckley wrote the following in his "Amsterdam Diary" in *Semiotext[e] SF* (Autonomedia, 1997):

> Good fiction is never preachy. It tells its truth only by inference and analogy. It uses the specific detail as its building block rather than the vague generalization. In my case it's usually humorous—no mistaking my stuff for the Platform Talk of the 6th Patriarch. But I do not try to be funny, I merely write as I write. . . . In the meantime I trust the voice I can never lose—my own . . . enjoying writing my story rather than looking forward to its completion.

SCIENCE FICTION AGAINST THE EMPIRE

I have a genetic predisposition for dialectic thinking. We can parse cyberpunk as a synthesizing form.

- *Cyber.* Discuss the ongoing global merger between humans and machines.
- *Punk.* Have the people be fully nonrobotic; have them be interested in sex, drugs, and rock 'n' roll. While you're at it, make the robots funky as well! Get in there and spray graffiti all over the corporate future.

As well as amping up the gnarliness, cyberpunk is concerned with the maintaining a high level of information in a story—where I'm using "information" in the technical computer-science sense of measuring how concise and nonredundant a message might be.

By way of having a high level of information, it's typical for cyberpunk novels to be written in a somewhat minimalist style, spewing out a rapid stream of characterization, ornamentation, plot twists, tech notions, and laconic dialog. The tendency is perhaps a bit similar to the way that punk rock arose as a reaction to arena rock, preferring a stripped-down style that was, in some ways, closer to the genre's roots.

When I moved to California in 1986, I fell in with the editors of the high-tech psychedelic magazine *Mondo 2000*, and they began referring to themselves as cyberpunks as well. They liked my notion of creating cultural artifacts with high levels of information, and their official T-shirt bore my slogan, "How fast are you? How dense?"

One of the less purely stylistic aspects of cyberpunk SF is that it's meant to be about the contemporary world. In this role, cyberpunk was trying to visualize and possibly to affect our rapidly oncoming future. If people's only concept of the future is *Star Trek*, then we're doomed to a bland fascism of the most corporate type. In a remark that I already mentioned above, Bruce Sterling said he wanted to get into those plastic futures and spray-paint them. One of the purposes of the cyberpunk novels was to show people by example that high-tech futures could be gnarly, with a nearly anarchist lack of any central control. The flourishing of the essentially unregulated World Wide Web shows that we were accurate in our dream.

I also want to say a bit about the countercultural aspects of the other modern SF movement I've been associated with: transrealism. My feeling is that a major tool in mass thought-control is the myth of consensus reality. Hand in hand with this myth goes the notion of a "normal person." A transrealist author creates characters who are realistically neurotic. One doesn't glorify the main character by making him or her unrealistically powerful, wise, or balanced. And the flipside of that is to humanize the villains.

There are no normal people—just look at your relatives, the people that you are in a position to know best. They're all weird at some level below the surface. Yet conventional fiction very commonly shows us normal people in a normal world. As long as you labor under the feeling that you are the only weirdo, then you feel weak and apologetic. You're eager to go along with the establishment, and a bit frightened to make waves—lest you be found out. Actual people are gnarly and unpredictable, this is why it is so important to use them as characters instead of the impossibly good and bad paperdolls of mass-culture.

The idea of breaking down consensus reality is important. This is where the tools of SF are particularly useful. Each mind is a reality unto itself. As long as people can be tricked into believing the reality of the ever-faster news-cycles, they can be herded about like sheep. The "president" threatens us with "nuclear war," and driven frantic by the fear of "death" we rush out to buy "consumer goods."

If you turn off your news feed you can reenter the human world. You eat something and go for a walk, with infinitely many thoughts and perceptions mingling with nature's infinitely many gnarly inputs.

Cyberpunk and transrealism are paths to a revolutionary SF.

CHANGING THE WORLD

Our society is made up of gnarly processes, and gnarly processes are inherently unpredictable.

My studies of cellular automata have made it very clear to me that it's easy for any kind of social system to generate gnarl. If we take a set of agents acting in parallel, we'll get unpredictable gnarl by repeatedly iterating almost any simple rule—such as "Earn an amount equal to the averages of your neighbors' incomes plus one—but when you reach a certain maximum level, go bankrupt and drop down to a minimum income."

Rules like this can generate wonderfully seething chaos. People sometimes don't want to believe that such a simple rule might account for the complexity of a living society. There's a tendency to think that a model with a more complicated definition will be a better fit for reality. But whatever richness comes out of a model is the result of a gnarly computation, which can occur in the very simplest of systems.

As I keep reiterating, the behavior of our gnarly society can't be predicted by computations that operate any faster than does real life. There are no tidy, handy-dandy rubrics for predicting or controlling emergent social processes like elections, the stock market, or consumer demand. Like a cellular automaton, society is a parallel computation, that is, a society is made up of individuals leading their own lives.

The good thing about a decentralized gnarly computing system is that it doesn't get stuck in some bad, minimally satisfactory state. The society's members are all working their hardest to improve things a bit like a swarm of ants tugging on a twig. Each ant is driven by its own responses to the surrounding cloud of communication pheromones. For a time, the ants may work at cross-purposes, but, as long as the society isn't stuck in a repetitive loop imposed from on high, they'll eventually happen upon success—like jiggling a key that turns a lock.

But how to reconcile the computational beauty of a gnarly, decentralized economy with the fact that many of those who advocate such a system are greedy plutocrats bent on screwing the middle class?

I think the problem is that, in practice, the multiple agents in a free-market economy are not of consummate size. Certain groups of agents clump together into powerful meta-agents. Think of a river of slushy, nearly frozen water. As long as the pieces of ice are of about the same size, the river will move in natural, efficient paths. But suppose that large ice floes form. The awkward motions of the floes disrupt any smooth currents, and, with their long borders, the floes have a propensity to grow larger and larger, reducing the responsiveness of the river still more.

In the same way, wealthy individuals or corporations can take on undue influence in a free market economy, acting as, in effect, unelected local governments. And this is where the watchdog role of a central government can be of use. The central government can act as a stick that reaches in to pound on the floes and break them into less disruptive sizes. This is, in fact, the reason why neocons and billionaires don't like the idea of a central government. When functioning properly, the government beats their cartels and puppet-parties to pieces.

Science fiction plays a role here. SF is one of the most trenchant present-day forms of satire. Harsh truths about our present-day society can be too inflammatory to express outright. But if they're dramatized within science-fictional worlds, vast numbers of citizens may be willing to absorb them.

For instance, Robert Heinlein's 1953 classic, *Revolt in 2100*, very starkly outlines what it can be like to live in a theocracy, and I'm sure that the book has made it a bit harder for such governments to take hold. John Shirley's 1988 story "Wolves of the Plateau" prefigured the eerie virtual violence of online hackerdom. And the true extent of the graft involved in George Bush's neocon invasion of Iraq comes into unforgettably sharp relief for anyone who reads William Gibson's 2007 *Spook Country*.

Backing up a little, it will have occurred to alert readers that a government that functions as a beating stick is nevertheless corruptible. It may well break up only certain kinds of organizations and turn a blind eye to those with the proper connections. Indeed this state of affairs is essentially inevitable given the vicissitudes of human nature.

Jumping up a level, we find this perennial consolation on the political front: any regime eventually falls. No matter how dark a nation's political times become, a change will come. A faction may think it rules a nation, but this is always an illusion. The eternally self-renewing gnarl of human behavior is impossible to control, and the times between regimes aren't normally so very long.

Sometimes it's not just single regimes that are the problem, but rather groups of nations that get into destructive and repetitive loops. I'm thinking of, in particular, the sequence of tit-for-tat reprisals that certain factions get into. Some loops of this nature have lasted my entire adult life.

But whether the problem is from a single regime or from a constellation of international relationships, one can remain confident that at some point gnarl will win out. Every pattern will break, every nightmare will end. Here is another place where SF has an influence. It helps people to visualize alternate realities, to understand that *things don't have to stay the same.*

One dramatic lesson we draw from SF simulations is that the most wide-ranging and extreme alterations can result from seemingly small changes. In general, society's coupled computations tend to produce events whose sizes have an unlimited range. This means that, inevitably, very large cataclysms will occasionally occur. Society is always in a gnarly state, which the writer Mark Buchanan refers to as "upheavable" in *Ubiquity: The Science of History . . . or Why the World Is Simpler Than You Think* (Crown, 2000 New York), 231–33.

Buchanan draws some conclusions about the flow of history that dovetail nicely with the notion of gnarly computation:

> History could in principle be like the growth of a tree, and follow a simple progression toward some mature and stable end point, as both Hegel and Karl Marx thought. In this case, wars and other tumultuous social events should grow less and less frequent as humanity approaches the stable society at the End of History. Or history might be like the movement of the Moon around the Earth, and be cyclic, as the historian Arnold Toynbee once suggested. He saw the rise and fall of civilizations as a process destined to repeat itself with regularity. Some economists believe they see regular cycles in economic activity, and a few political scientists suspect that such cycles drive a correspondingly regular rhythm in the outbreak of wars. Of course, history might instead be completely random, and present no perceptible patterns whatsoever . . .
>
> But this list is incomplete . . . The [gnarly] critical state bridges the conceptual gap between the regular

and the random. The pattern of change to which it leads through its rise of factions and wild fluctuations is neither truly random nor easily predicted. . . . It does not seem normal and lawlike for long periods of calm to be suddenly and sporadically shattered by cataclysm, and yet it is. This is, it seems, the ubiquitous character of the world.

In his *Foundation* series, Isaac Asimov depicts a universe in which the future is to some extent regular and predictable, rather than being gnarly. His mathematician character Hari Seldon has created a technique called "psychohistory" that allows him to foretell the large-scale motions of society. This is fine for an SF series, but in the real world, it seems not to be possible.

One of the more intriguing observations regarding history is that, from time to time a society seems to undergo a sea change, a discontinuity, a revolution—think of the Renaissance, the Reformation, the Industrial Revolution, the Sixties, or the coming of the Web. In these rare cases it appears as if the underlying rules of the system have changed.

Although the day-to-day progress of the system may be in any case unpredictable, there's a limited range of possible values that the system actually hits. In the interesting cases, these possible values lie on a fractal shape in some higher-dimensional space of possibilities—this shape is what chaos theory calls a strange attractor.

Looking at the surf near a spit at the beach, you'll notice that certain water patterns recur over and over—perhaps a double-crowned wave on the right, perhaps a bubbling pool of surge beside the rock, perhaps a high-flown spray of spume off the front of the rock. This range of patterns is a strange attractor. When the tide is lower or the wind is different, the waves will run through a different repertoire—they'll be moving on a different strange attractor.

During any given historical period, a society has a kind of strange attractor. A limited number of factions fight over power, a limited number of social roles are available for the citizens, a limited range of ideas are in the air. And then, suddenly, everything changes, and after the change there's a new set of options—society has moved to a new strange attractor. Although there's been no change in the underlying rule for the social computation, some parameter has altered so that the range of currently possible behaviors has changed.

Society's switches to new chaotic attractors are infrequently occurring zigs and zags generated by one and the same underlying and eternal gnarly social computation. The basic underlying computation involves such immutable facts as the human drives to eat, find shelter, and live long enough to reproduce. From such humble rudiments doth history's great tapestry emerge endlessly various, eternally the same.

I mentioned that SF helps us to highlight the specific quirks of our society at a given time. It's also the case that SF shows us how our world could change to a radically different set of strange attractors. One wonders, for instance, if the World Wide Web would have arisen in its present form if it hadn't been for the popularity of Tolkien and of cyberpunk science fiction. Very many of the programmers were reading both of these sets of novels.

It seems reasonable to suppose that Tolkien helped steer programmers towards the Web's odd, niche-rich, fantasy-land architecture. And surely the cyberpunk novels instilled the idea of having an anarchistic Web with essentially no centralized controllers at all. The fact that that the Web turned out to be so free and ubiquitous seems almost too good to be true. I speculate that it's thanks to Tolkien and to cyberpunk that our culture made its way to the new strange attractor where we presently reside.

In short, SF and fantasy are more than forms of entertainment. They're tools for changing the world.

RAPTURE IN SPACE

DENNY BLEVINS WAS A DREAMER who didn't like to think. Drugs and no job put his head in just the right place for this. If at all possible, he liked to get wired and spend the day lying on his rooming house mattress and looking out the window at the sky. On clear days he could watch his eyes' phosphenes against the bright blue; and on cloudy days he'd dig the clouds' drifty motions and boiling edges. One day he realized his window-dirt was like a constant noise-hum in the system, so he knocked out the pane that he usually looked through. The sky was even better then, and when it rained he could watch the drops coming in. At night he might watch the stars, or he might get up and roam the city streets for deals.

His dad, whom he hadn't seen in several years, died that April. Denny flew out to the funeral. His big brother Allen was there, with Dad's insurance money. Turned out they got $15K apiece.

"Don't squander it, Denny," said Allen, who was an English teacher. "Time's winged chariot for no man waits! You're getting older and it's time you found a career. Go to school and learn something. Or buy into a trade. Do something to make Dad's soul proud."

"I will," said Denny, feeling defensive. Instead of talking in clear he used the new cyberslang. "I'll get so cashy and so starry so zip you won't believe it, Allen. I'll get a tunebot, start a motion, and cut a choicey vid. Denny in the Clouds with Clouds. Untense, bro, I've got plex ideas."

When Denny got back to his room he got a new sound system and a self-playing electric guitar. And scored a lot of dope and food-packs. The days went by; the money dwindled to $9K. Early in June the phone rang.

"Hello, Denny Blevins?" The voice was false and crackly.

"Yes!" Denny was glad to get a call from someone besides Allen. It seemed like lately Allen was constantly calling him up to nag.

"Welcome to the future. I am Phil, a phonebot cybersystem designed to contact consumer prospects. I would like to tell about the on-line possibilities open to you. Shall I continue?"

"Yes," said Denny.

It turned out the "Phil the phonebot" was a kind of computerized phone salesman. The phonebot was selling phonebots which you, the consumer prospect, could use to sell phonebots to others. It was—though Denny didn't realize this—a classic Ponzi pyramid scheme, like a chain letter, or like those companies which sell people franchises to sell franchises to sell franchises to sell . . .

The phonebot had a certain amount of interactivity. It asked a few yes/no questions; and whenever Denny burst in with some comment, it would pause, say, "That's right, Denny! But listen to the rest!" and continue. Denny was pleased to hear his name so often. Alone in his room, week after week, he'd been feeling his reality fade. Writing original songs for the guitar was harder than he'd expected. It would be nice to have a robot friend. At the end, when Phil asked for his verdict, Denny said, "Okay, Phil, I want you. Come to my rooming-house tomorrow and I'll have the money."

The phonebot was not the arm-waving clanker that Denny, in his ignorance, had imagined. It was, rather, a flat metal box that plugged right into the wall phone-socket. The box had a slot for an electronic directory, and a speaker for talking to its owner. It told Denny he could call it Phil; all the phonebots were named Phil. The basic phonebot sales spiel was stored in the Phil's memory, though you could change the patter if you wanted. You could, indeed, use the phonebot to sell things other than phonebots.

The standard salespitch lasted five minutes, and one minute was allotted to the consumer's responses. If everyone answered, listened, and responded, the phonebot could process ten prospects per hour, and one hundred twenty in a 9 a.m. – 9 p.m. day! The whole system cost nine thousand dollars, though as soon as you bought one and joined the pyramid, you could get more of them for six. Three thousand dollars profit for each phonebot your phonebot could sell! If you sold, say, one a day, you'd make better than $100K a year!

The electronic directory held all the names and numbers in the city; and each morning it would ask Denny who he wanted to try today. He could select the numbers on the day's calling list on the basis of neighborhood, last name, family size, type of business, and so on.

The first day, Denny picked a middle-class suburb and told Phil to call all the childless married couples there.

Young folks looking for an opportunity! Denny set the speaker so he could listen to people's responses. It was not encouraging.

"*click*"

"No . . . *click*"

"*click*"

"This kilp ought to be illegal . . . *click*"

"*click*"

"Get a job, you bizzy dook . . . *click*"

"Of all the . . . *click*"

"Again? *click*"

Most people hung up so fast that Phil was able to make some thousand unsuccessful contacts in less than ten hours. Only seven people listened through the whole message and left comments at the end; and six of these people seemed to be bedridden or crazy. The seventh had a phonebot she wanted to sell cheap.

Denny tried different phoning strategies—rich people, poor people, people with two sevens in their phone number, and so on. He tried different kinds of salespitches—bossy ones, ingratiating ones, curt ones, ethnic-accent ones, etc. He made up a salespitch that offered businesses the chance to rent Phil to do phone advertising for them.

Nothing worked. It got to be depressing sitting in his room watching Phil fail—it was like having Willy Loman for his roommate. The machine made little noises, and unless Denny took a *lot* of dope, he had trouble relaxing out into the sky. The empty food-packs stank.

Two more weeks, and all the money, food, and dope were gone. Right after he did the last of the dope, Denny recorded a final sales-pitch:

"Uh . . . hi. This is Phil the prophet at 1801 Eye Street. I eye I . . . I'm out of money and I'd rather not have to . . . uh . . . leave my room. You send me money for . . . uh . . . food and I'll give God your name. Dope's rail, too."

Phil ran that on random numbers for two days with no success. Denny came down into deep hunger. Involuntary detox. If his dad had left much more money, Denny might have died, holed up in that room. Good old Dad. Denny trembled out into the street and got a job working counter in a Greek coffee shop called the KoDo. It was okay; there was plenty of food, and he didn't have to watch Phil panhandling.

As Denny's strength and sanity came back, he remembered sex. But he didn't know any girls. He took Phil off panhandling and put him onto propositioning numbers in the young working-girl neighborhoods.

"Hi, are you a woman? I'm Phil, sleek robot for a whippy young man who's ready to get under. Make a guess and he'll mess. Leave your number and state your need; he's fuff-looking and into sleaze."

This message worked surprisingly well. The day after he started it up, Denny came home to find four enthusiastic responses stored on Phil's chips. Two of the responses seemed to be from men, and one of the women's voice sounded old . . . *really old*. The fourth response was from "Silke."

"Hi, desperado, this is Silke. I like your machine. Call me."

Phil had Silke's number stored, of course, so Denny called her right up. Feeling shy, he talked through Phil, using the machine as voder to make his voice sound weird. After all, Phil was the one who knew her.

"Hello?" Cute, eager, practical, strange.

"Silke? This is Phil. Denny's talking through me. You want to interface?"

"Like where?"

"My room?"

"Is it small? It sounds like your room is small. I like small rooms."

"You got it. 1801 Eye Street, Denny'll be in front of the building."

"What do you look like, Denny?"

"Tall, thin, teeth when I grin, which is lots. My hair's peroxide blond on top. I'll wear my X-shirt."

"Me too. See you in an hour."

Denny put on his X-shirt—a T-shirt with a big silk screen picture of his genitalia—and raced down to the KoDo to beg Spiros, the boss, for an advance on his wages.

"Please, Spiros, I got a date."

The shop was almost empty, and Spiros was sitting at the counter watching a pay-vid porno show on his pocket TV. He glanced over at Denny, all decked out in his X-shirt, and pulled two fifties out of his pocket.

"Let me know how she come."

Denny spent one fifty on two Fiesta food-packs and some wine: the other fifty went for a capsule of snap-crystals from a street vendor. He was back in front of his rooming-house in plenty of time. Ten minutes, and there came Silke, with a great big pink crotch-shot printed onto her T-shirt. She looked giga good.

For the first instant they stood looking at each other's X-shirts, and then they shook hands.

"I'm Denny Blevins. I got some food and wine and snap here, if you want to go up." Denny was indeed tall and thin, and toothy when he grinned. His mouth was very wide. His hair was long and dark in back, and short and blond on top. He wore red rhinestone earrings, his semierect X-shirt, tight black plastic pants, and fake leopard fur shoes. His arms were muscular and veiny, and he moved them a lot when he talked.

"Go up and get under," smiled Silke. She was medium height, and wore her straw-like black hair in a bouffant. She had fine, hard features. She'd appliquéd pictures of monster eyes to her eyelids, and she wore white dayglo lipstick. Beneath her sopping wet X-shirt image, she wore a tight, silvered jumpsuit with cutouts. On her feet she had roller skates with lights in the wheels.

"Oxo," said Denny.

"Wow," said Silke.

Up in the room they got to know each other. Denny showed Silke his phonebot and his sound system, pretended to start to play his guitar and to then decide not to, and told about some of the weird things he'd seen in the sky, looking out that broken pane. Silke, as it turned out, was a pay-vid sex dancer come here from West Virginia. She talked mostly in clear, but she was smart, and she liked to get wild, but only with the right kind of guy. Sex dancer didn't mean hooker and she was, she assured Denny, clean. She had a big dream she wasn't quite willing to tell him yet.

"Come on," he urged, popping the autowave food-packs open. "Decode."

"Ah, I don't know, Denny. You might think I'm skanky."

They sat side by side on Denny's mattress and ate the pasty food with plastic spoons. It was good. It was good to have another person in the room here.

"Silke," said Denny when they finished eating, "I'd been thinking Phil was kilp. Dook null. But if he got you here it was worth it. Seems I just need tech to relate, you wave?"

Silke threw the empty foodtrays on the floor and gave Denny a big kiss. They went ahead and fuffed. It seemed like it had been a while for both of them. Skin all over, soft, warm, touch, kiss, lick, smell, good, skin.

Afterwards, Denny opened the capsule of snap and they split it. You put the stuff on your tongue, it sputtered and popped, and you breathed in the freebase fumes. Fab rush. Out through the empty window pane they could see the moon and two stars stronger than the city lights.

"Out there," said Silke, her voice fast and shaky from the snap. "That's my dream. If we hurry, Denny, we can be the first people to have sex in space. They'd remember us forever. I've been thinking about it, and there was always missing links, but you and Phil are it. We'll get in the shuttlebox—it's a room like this—and go up. We get up there and make videos of us getting under, and—this is my new flash—we use Phil to sell the vids to pay for the trip. You wave?"

Denny's long, maniacal smile curled across his face. The snap was still crackling on his tongue. "Stuzzadelic! Nobody's fuffed in space yet? None of those gawks who've used the shuttlebox?"

"They might have, but not for the record. But if we scurry we'll be the famous first forever. We'll be starry."

"Oxo, Silke." Denny's voice rose with excitement. "Are you there, Phil?"

"Yes, Denny."

"Got a new pitch. In clear."

"Proceed."

"Hi, this is Denny." He nudged the naked girl next to him.

"And this is Silke."

"We're doing a live fuff-vid we'd like to show you."

"It's called *Rapture in Space*. It's the very first X-rated love film from outer space."

"Zero gravity," said Denny, reaching over to whang on his guitar.

"Endless fun."

"Mindless pleasure." *Whang*.

"Out near the sun." Silke nuzzled his neck and moaned stagily. "Oh, Denny, oh, darling, it's . . ."

"RAPTURE IN SPACE! Satisfaction guaranteed. This is bound to be a collector's item; the very first live sex video from space. A full ninety minutes of unbelievable null-gee action, with great Mother Earth in the background, tune in for only fifty . . ."

"More, Denny," wailed Silke, who was now grinding herself against him with some urgency. "More!"

Whang. "Only one hundred dollars, and going up fast. To order, simply leave your card number after the beep."

"*Beep!*"

Phil got to work the next morning, calling numbers of businesses where lots of men worked. The orders poured in. Lacking a business-front by which to cash the credit orders, Denny enlisted Spiros, who quickly set up KoDo Space Rapture Enterprises. For managing the business, Spiros only wanted 15 percent and some preliminary tapes of Denny and Silke in action. For another 45 percent, Silke's porno pay-vid employers—an outfit known as XVID—stood ready to distribute the show. Dreaming of this day, Silke had already bought her own cameras. She and Denny practiced a lot, getting their moves down. Spiros agreed that the rushes looked good. Denny went ahead and reserved the shuttlebox for a trip in mid-July.

The shuttlebox was a small passenger module that could be loaded into the space shuttle for one of its weekly trips up to orbit and back. A trip for two cost $100K. Denny bought electronic directories for cities across the country, and set Phil to working twenty hours a day. He averaged fifty sales a day, and by launch time, Silke and Denny had enough to pay everyone off, and then some.

But this was just the beginning. Three days before the launch, the news services picked up on the *Rapture in Space* plan, and everything went crazy. There was no way for a cheap box like Phil to process the orders anymore. Denny and Silke had to give XVID anther 15 percent of the action, and let them handle the tens of thousands of orders. It was projected that *Rapture in Space* would pull an audience share of 7 percent—which is a lot of people. Even more money came in the form of fat contracts for two product endorsements: SPACE RAPTURE, the cosmic eroscent for high-flyers, and RAPT SHIELD, an antiviral lotion for use by sexual adventurers. XVID and the advertisers privately wished that Denny and Silke were a bit more . . . *upscale*-looking, but they were the two who had the tiger by the tail.

Inevitably, some of the Christian Party congressmen tried to have Denny and Silke enjoined from making an XVID broadcast from aboard the space shuttle, which was, after all, government property. But for 5 percent of the gross, a fast-thinking lawyer was able to convince a hastily convened Federal court that, insofar as *Rapture in Space* was being codecast to the XVID dish and cabled thence only to paying subscribers, the show was a form of constitutionally protected free speech, in no way different from a live-sex show in a private club.

So the great day came. Naked save for a drenching of Space Rapture eroscent, Silke and Denny waved goodbye and stepped into their shuttle-box. It was shaped like a two-meter-thick letter D, with a rounded floor, and with a big picture window set into the flat ceiling. A crane loaded the shuttlebox into the bay of the space shuttle along with some satellites, missiles, building materials, etc. A worker dogged all the stuff down, and then the baydoors closed. Silke and Denny wedged themselves into their puttylike floor. Blast off—roar, shudder, push, clunk, roar some more.

Then they were floating. The baydoors swung open, and the astronauts got to work with their retractable arms and space tools. Silke and Denny were busy, too. They set up the cameras, and got their little antenna locked in on the XVID dish. They started broadcasting right away— some of the *Rapture in Space* subscribers had signed up for the whole live protocols in addition to the ninety-minute show that Silke and Denny were scheduled to put on in . . .

"Only half an hour, Denny," said Silke. "Only thirty minutes till we go on." She was crouched over the sink, douching, and vacuuming the water back up. As fate would have it, she was menstruating. She hadn't warned anyone about it.

Denny felt cold and sick to his stomach. XVID had scheduled their show right after take-off because other-wise—with all the news going on—people might forget about it. But right now he didn't feel like fuffing at all, let alone getting under. Every time he touched something, or even breathed, his whole body moved.

"All clean now," sang Silke. "No one can tell, not even you."

There was a rapping on their window—one of the astronauts, a jolly jock woman named Judy. She grinned through her helmet and gave them a high sign. The astronauts thought the *Rapture in Space* show was a great idea; it would make people think about them in new, more interesting ways.

"I talked to Judy before the launch," said Silke, waving back. "She said to watch out for the rebound." She floated to Denny and began fondling him. "Ten minutes, starman."

Outside the window, Judy was a shiny form against Earth's great marbled curve. *The clouds*, Denny realized, *I'm seeing the clouds from on top*. His genitals were warming to Silke's touch. He tongued a snap crystal out of a crack between his teeth and bit it open. Inhale. The clouds. Silke's touch. He was hard, thank God, he was hard. This was going to be all right.

The cameras made a noise to signal the start of the main transmission, and Denny decided to start by planting a kiss on Silke's mouth. He bumped her shoulder and she started to drift away. She tightened her grip on his penis and led him along after her. It hurt, but not too unpleasantly. She landed on her back, on the padded floor, and guided Denny right into her vagina. Smooth and warm. Good. Denny pushed into her and . . . *rebound*.

He flew, rapidly and buttocks first, up to the window. He had hold of Silke's armpit and she came with him. She got her mouth over his penis for a second, which was good, but then her body spun around, and she slid toothrakingly off him, which was very bad.

Trying to hold a smile, Denny stole a look at the clock. Three minutes. *Rapture in Space* had been on for three minutes now. Eighty-seven minutes to go.

It was another bruising half hour or so until Denny and Silke began to get the hang of spacefuffing. And then it was fun. For a long time they hung in midair, with Denny in Silke, and Silke's legs around his waist, just gently jogging, but moaning and throwing their heads around for the camera. Actually, the more they hammed it up, the better it felt. Autosuggestion.

Denny stared and stared at the clouds to keep from coming, but finally he had to pull out for a rest. To keep things going they did rebounds for a while. Silke would lie spread-eagled on the floor, and Denny would kind of leap down on her; both of them adjusting their pelvises for a bullseye. She'd sink into the cushions, then rebound them both up. It got better and better. Silke curled up into a ball and impaled herself on Denny's shaft. He wedged himself against the wall with his feet and one hand and used his other hand to spin her around and around, bobbin on his spindle. Denny lay on the floor and Silke did leaps onto him. They kissed and licked each other all over, and from every angle. The time was almost up.

For the finale, they went back to midair fuffing; arms and legs wrapped around each other; one camera aimed at their faces, and one camera aimed at their genitalia. They hit a rhythm where they always pushed just as hard as each other and it action/reaction cancelled out, hard and harder, with big Earth out the window, yes, the air full of their smells, yes, the only sound the sound of their ragged breathing, yes, now, NOW AAAHHHHHHH!!!!

Denny kind of fainted there, and forgot to slide out for the come-shot. Silke went blank, too, and they just floated, linked like puzzle pieces for five or ten minutes. It made a great finale for the *Rapture in Space* show, really much more convincing than the standard sperm spurt.

Two days later, and they were back on Earth, with the difference that they were now, as Denny had hoped, cashy and starry. People recognized them everywhere, and looked at them funny, often asking for a date. They did some interviews, some more endorsements and they got an XVID contract to host a monthly spacefuff variety show.

Things were going really good until Denny got a tumor.

"It's a dooky little kilp down in my bag," he complained to Silke. "Feel it."

Sure enough, there was a one-centimeter lump in Denny's scrotum. Silke wanted him to see a doctor, but he kept stalling. He was afraid they'd run a blood test and get on his case about drugs. Some things were still illegal.

A month went by and the lump was the size of an orange.

"It's so gawky you can see it through my pants," complained Denny. "It's giga ouch and I can't cut a vid this way."

But he still wouldn't go to the doctor. What with all the snap he could buy, and with his new cloud telescope, Denny didn't notice what was going on in his body most of the time. He was happy to miss the next few XVID dates. Silke hosted them alone.

Three more months and the lump was like a small watermelon. When Denny came down one time and noticed that the tumor was moving he really got worried

"Silke! It's alive! The thing in my bag is alive! Aaauuugh!"

Silke paid a doctor two thousand dollars to come to their apartment. The doctor was a bald, dignified man with a white beard. He examined Denny's scrotum for a long time, feeling, listening, and watching the tumor's occasional twitches. Finally he pulled the covers back over Denny and sat down. He regarded Silke and Denny in silence for quite some time.

"Decode!" demanded Denny. "What the kilp we got running here?"

"You're pregnant," said the doctor. "Four months into it, I'd say."

The quickening fetus gave another kick and Denny groaned. He knew it was true. "But how?"

The doctor steepled his fingers. "I . . . I saw *Rapture in Space*. There were certain signs to indicate that your uh partner was menstruating?"

"Check."

"Menstruation, as you must know, involves the discharge of the unfertilized ovum along with some discarded uterine tissues. I would speculate that after your ejaculation the ovum became wedged in your meatus. The slit at the tip of your penis. It is conceivable that under weightless conditions the sperm's flagella could have driven the now-fertilized ovum into your vas deferens. The ovum implanted itself in the bloodrich tissues there and developed into a fetus."

"I want an abortion."

"No!" protested Silke. "That's our baby, Denny. You're already almost half done carrying it. It'll be lovely for us . . . and just think of the publicity!"

"Uh . . ." said Denny, reaching for his bag of dope.

"No more drugs," said the doctor, snatching the bag. "Except for the ones I give you." He broke into a broad, excited smile. "This will make medical history."

And indeed it did. The doctor designed Denny a kind of pouch in which he could carry his pregnant scrotum, and Denny made a number of video appearances, not all of them X-rated. He spoke on the changing roles of the sexes, and he counted the days till delivery. In the public's mind, Denny became the symbol of a new recombining of sex with life and love. In Denny's own mind, he finally became a productive and worthwhile person. The baby was a flawless girl, delivered by a modified Caesarian section.

Sex was never the same again.

NOTES

Dennis Poague, a.k.a. Sta-Hi, was the inspiration for this story; he really did spend his inheritance on a phoning machine. I wrote this story shortly after seeing the IMAX movie *The Dream Is Alive*, which featured pictures of the sexy astronaut Judy Resnick sleeping in zero-gee. The *Challenger* shuttle blew up with Judy in it a few months later, definitively deep-sixing whatever slim chance "Rapture in Space" had of getting into a normal SF magazine.

Semiotext[e] SF was an anthology which Peter Lamborn Wilson and I coedited. Originally we'd planned to call the book *Bad Brains*, but Peter felt doing this would conflict with the band of the same name. At the time, Peter rented an apartment upstairs from the apartment of my friend Eddie Marritz in New York City, which is how I happened to meet him. Eddie appears in the story "Tales of Houdini," in the memoir "Drugs and Live Sex—NYC 1980," and in the novel *Master of Space and Time*.

A funny Dennis story. When we moved to San Jose, it turned out Dennis lived here, so we started getting together a lot. I was supposed to give a reading at an annual San Jose SF convention called Bay Con in 1987, and the day before the reading I was in a bicycle accident and had a huge black eye. I didn't want to appear in public looking so bad, so I gave Dennis my manuscript of *As Above, So Below* and told him to do the reading. I figured he would enjoy this free taste of fame, and I was right—remember that one of *Software* Sta-Hi's big obsessions is how to become famous.

Although I'd already made friends with the San Francisco SF writers, none of the fans knew at Bay Con knew what I looked like, so when Dennis appeared in a corduroy jacket and read my story, they assumed he was me. The funny thing was, when I came and did my own reading at Bay Con a year later, several people came up to me and said, "You know, I saw your reading last year and it was wonderful. You made the material so fresh and new . . . it was like you'd never even read it before!"

"LOAD ON THE MIRACLES AND KEEP A STRAIGHT FACE"

RUDY RUCKER INTERVIEWED BY TERRY BISSON

Your new book, Nested Scrolls, *is an autobiography. Does that mean you've run out of ideas?*

I feel like I always have new ideas, but certainly some of them are beginning to look a little familiar. I get SF ideas by extrapolating, from speculating, and from imagining surreal juxtapositions.

In 2008, I had a cerebral hemorrhage—a vein burst in my brain and I nearly died. Coming out of that, I decided that I'd better write my autobio while I still had time.

One of my goals in writing *Nested Scrolls* was to get an idea of the story arc of my life—as if I were looking back on a novel. My conclusions? I searched for ultimate reality, and I found contentment in creativity. I tried to scale the heights of science, and I found my calling in mathematics and in science fiction. I was a loner, I found love, I became a family man. When I was a kid, I felt like an ugly duckling, and over the years I grew into grace—thanks in large measure to my dear wife, Sylvia.

Aren't novels a rather messy exercise for a mathematician? Do you have the whole thing in RAM when you start, or do you make it up as you go along?

In some ways mathematics resembles novel-writing. In math you start with some oddball axioms and see what theorems you can deduce from them. You have very little control over the course that your reasoning takes. In novel-writing, you start with an outré scenario and see what kind of plot emerges from the situation. Here again, the details of your work tends to come as something of a surprise.

In science fiction, it's useful to be able to think logically, which is something that comes naturally for a mathematician.

But of course SF novels are more than logical exercises, and that's why I love writing them. I like the possibility of expressing myself at various levels—sometimes it isn't until later that I realize something I've written has to do with some deep obsession of mine.

Frek and the Elixir *has been described as a YA (young adult) novel. Is this because it has a kid as a protagonist, or because only kids can understand it?*

Tor didn't actually market this book as YA, although that might have been a good idea. When YA books catch on, they can sell very well. But in *Frek*, I wasn't fully focused on teenage problems, as is usually the case in YA books. Although the thirteen-year-old Frek has some abandonment issues with his father, he's also dealing with the social issue of many species becoming extinct.

In order to give Frek and the *Elixir* a classy feel, I modeled the book on the "monomyth" template described in Joseph Campbell's classic *The Hero with a Thousand Faces*. Campbell's archetypal myth includes seventeen stages. By combining two pairs of stages, I ended up with fifteen chapters for *Frek*.

I'd like to revisit the world of *Frek* and write a sequel. I liked those characters, especially the flying cuttlefish called Professor Bumby. I had him as a professor in my abstract algebra course in grad school.

Your webzine Flurb *reads like a who's who of outside-the-box SF writers. Who would you most like to get an unsolicited manuscript from, living or dead?*

I've had a lot of fun editing *Flurb*, and as a personal matter, it's convenient to have a magazine which will always publish my stories. I sleep with the editor's wife, as I like to say.

I started with asking my old cyberpunk friends to contribute, but over time I'm getting more over-the-transom material from younger writers. Regarding your question, I'd be happy to get manuscripts from Robert Sheckley, Philip K. Dick, Thomas Pynchon, or Jack Kerouac. It's not so well known that the Beats were very interested in writing SF, and they talked about it a lot. They viewed SF as an indigenous American art form, along the lines of rock 'n' roll or jazz.

If you look at it in a certain way, William Burroughs's novel *Naked Lunch* is an SF novel. But there's a certain goody-goody nerd element among SF people that tends not to want to acknowledge that.

What is Time? Seriously.

Kurt Gödel, the smartest man I ever met, claimed that the passage of time is an illusion, a kind of grain built into the fabric of our reality. To the extent that we can sense Eternity, it's present in the immediate Now moment. Another point to make is that, insofar as time is real, it's like a fluid we swim around in. As John Updike puts it, "Time is our element, not a mistaken invader."

Okay, I'm regurgitating quotes there. A simpler answer: time is breath. Does that answer your question?

No. You seem to have a knack for running into famous characters: Anselm Hollo, Martin Gardner, Gödel, Wolfram? If you were forming a band, which would play lead guitar? Would Turing be in the band?

I'd probably like to be lead singer, like I was in my short-lived punk band, the Dead Pigs, in 1982. In this case I'd choose Johnny Ramone as lead guitarist. If I had a better voice, I'd want to work with Frank Zappa, but in reality I don't think Frank would let me sing. Maybe I could play kazoo. And of course I'd be happy singing with Keith Richards or Muddy Waters.

Being in a band was one of the more enjoyable things I've done. Much of my career has consisted of mathematics, computer hacking, and writing. These are solitary activities, so it was fun for me to be in a band and do something in group. Come to think of it, that's another reason I like editing my webzine *Flurb*.

I don't think Alan Turing was all that interested in music, but I'd enjoy having him as a friend. He was interested in writing science fiction, as a matter of fact, and he also had an interest in heavy philosophical trips. I'm currently writing a novel with the working title *The Turing Chronicles*, which centers on a love affair between Turing and William Burroughs.

I feel like I'm getting to know Turing and Burroughs via the process of writing about them and maintaining internal emulations of them. I've often done this in the past—I call it "twinking" someone. I twinked the mathematician Georg Cantor in my novel *White Light*, Edgar Allen Poe in *The Hollow Earth*, and the painter Peter Bruegel in my historical novel about his life, *As Above, So Below*. Bruegel was the best. He's a wonderful man.

Do you ever write longhand? Do you own a pencil?

In my back pocket I almost always carry a blank sheet of printing paper folded in four. I write ideas down on the paper, and when I get home, I type the notes into my computer; generally I've got a notes document going for whatever book I'm working on. I do write longhand on my pocket notes paper. Sometimes I can't read the writing later on. I used to take copy-books on trips with me and write longer passages in them, but now I almost always travel with a laptop.

Does anyone ever "own" a pencil? They're just things you rummage for, briefly use, and immediately lose. But now and then, if I have a pencil, I might use it to draw something on my pocket square of paper. More commonly I use a Pilot P-700 pen, preferably Extra Fine. I've been using these for going on fifteen years now, and I worry about them going out of production. Every now and then I buy a big stash of them, like fifty or a hundred.

You sometimes collaborate on short stories, with Paul DiFilippo, Marc Laidlaw, John Shirley, Bruce Sterling, Eileen Gunn, even myself. Is this laziness or ambition?

As I already mentioned, writing is a somewhat lonely activity, so I enjoy collaborating on stories. There's no reason not to. The thing about short stories is that they're really hard to sell, at least for me. There's only a very small number of story markets, and often I end up having to publish a story in *Flurb*. And even if I do sell a story, it pays very little, and it can take several years before the story appears. It's not a satisfying market at all. So I might as well have some fun in the writing process by collaborating.

When you write together, it's something like a musical collaboration, a spontaneous give and take. I find that, in order to blend the prose, I tend to imitate the other author's style. Like the way that actors in Woody Allen movies usually seem to talk like Woody.

If you could spend twenty-four hours in any city on the planet, with money in your pocket, which would it be?

First of all, I'm not going for just twenty-four hours. Why travel so far and turn right around? That's idiocy. I'm staying for at least four days and maybe a week.

As for destinations—I'm a huge fan of New York City. I love the noise—you hear it as soon as you get out of the airport, a filigree of sirens overlaid onto a mighty roar. The museums are great, and I know a fair number of cozy, inexpensive restaurants filled with hipsters and city slickers. I'd catch some ballet, and maybe a rock band. Just walking the streets in NYC is a great entertainment as well. And as long as you're paying, Terry, maybe I'll stay at the refurbished Gramercy Park Hotel.

I'd love to spend a week in Koror, a funky town in the archipelago of Palau. I'd go diving, riding a Sam's Tours boat out to the Blue Corner, which is perhaps the greatest dive spot in the world. I'd probably stay at the Palau Royal Resort, and I'd snorkel at the hotel beach, admiring the richly patterned mantles of the giant clams.

A lot of scenes in my SF novels are drawn from my dive experiences. SCUBA is really the closest thing we have to floating in outer space and to visiting alien worlds. Well, NYC is fairly alien as well. Life in the hive.

Your film career was cut short after The Manual of Evasion. *What went wrong?*

Well, you're talking about the acting part of my film career. *The Manual of Evasion* movie was also called *LX94*, as it was made in Lisbon in 1994. Terence McKenna and Robert Anton Wilson starred with me, and some excerpts are online, although the complete movie is hard to find. The director of that movie, Edgar Pêra, is a really good guy. I went to visit him in Lisbon again in the summer of 2011.

In terms of movies, what I'd really like is for one of my novels to be made into a film. We came close with *Software*. It was under option to Phoenix Pictures for a decade and they paid for about ten screenplays, none by me. *Master of Space and Time* was another near-miss. Michel Gondry wanted to direct, Jim Carrey and Jack

Black were going to star, and Daniel Clowes wrote a script. A dream team.

But the producers didn't want to lay out the money. It still seems like the big-money people find my work a little too gnarly. Maybe I'm ahead of my time. That could change at some point. But it's not a prospect I obsess on. I joke that they can't make any of my novels into movies until they've made ever single one of Phillip K. Dick's novels and short stories into a film. And that's going to take awhile.

You are (in my mind, at least) a "hard SF" writer in that the machinery of your work is always math and physics. What do you have against wizards?

I don't like it in a fantastic story when there are a large number of unexplained loose ends. In the context of TV series, I think of *The X-Files* or *Lost*, where the scriptwriters are continually piling on new complications, and none of the earlier mysteries are being solved, and the narrator just gives you these big-eyed woo-woo significant looks.

It isn't really that hard to devote a little effort and figure out a logical framework for the story you want to tell. For a professional SF writer, it might take a day. But for some reason, TV and movie people are literally unable to do this—and they're unwilling to hire an SF writer as a consultant. They'll spend a hundred million on the effects, but they won't give some poor SF vet a hundred K so the story makes sense. I don't understand it.

Back to books, my feeling is that you can be just as logical in a fantasy story as in a science-fiction story. But there seems to be a convention in fantasy that you're not expected to cash the checks that you write. You do any old thing, and then move on to something else and you never circle back. I guess I care more about logic than most people do. Must have something to do with the PhD in mathematics.

My most recent novel, *Jim and the Flims*, is to some extent a fantasy story—a large part of it is set in the afterworld, and my characters are battling with otherworldly beings who are basically demons. But I found it natural to think of some pseudoscientific explanations for the goings-on, and working the logic into the story made me feel more comfortable.

What drew you into math, chaos or order? What drew you into literature?

From the start I liked math's tidiness and power— the numbers and the geometric diagrams. As for literature, I always loved reading and traveling to other worlds. I read science fiction as a boy, and Beat literature in high school. I came to appreciate the radical, countercultural aspects of literature as well.

I wanted to major in English in college, but my father nagged me that I should major in something hard that I couldn't learn on my own. He made the point that I could read novels without taking classes about them. So I decided to major in physics. But then I didn't take the right courses freshman year, and only the math option was open for me. I was okay with that because I found math easy. If you understand what's going on in math, you don't have to memorize very much. Most of what you need to know follows logically from a few basic principles. And

I like that math has a lot of gnarl—chaotic patterns that emerge from seeming order.

When I finished college in 1967, I had the option of going to fight in Viet Nam or going to grad school, and I picked grad school. I'd been a very poor student in college, and I only had a C average. So I had some trouble getting into a PhD program. As it happened, I married my wife Sylvia the week after graduation, and Rutgers University was eager to have her enter their graduate French program. The French chairman put in a word with the math chairman, and they let me in. I ended up getting my doctorate at Rutgers, a PhD in mathematical logic. And by the time I was done, my average was more like an A than a C. I'd finally found some course material that interested me.

I wrote my first novel, *Spacetime Donuts*, around 1976. I was amped up from having seen the Rolling Stones play live in Buffalo, New York. Ultimately, writing was to be my real career, and teaching my day job.

As it happened, I switched from teaching math to teaching computer science when my family and I moved to San Jose, California, in 1986. This was a good move for me. It meant I got to ride a twenty-year wave of computer science, from PCs up through the Web. I never took a single course in computer science, but eventually I taught most of them. I enjoyed the hands-on, experimental nature of the subject, and some of it permanently changed the way I think.

Are you prepared for the Singularity?

I have complicated thoughts about the so-called Singularity. First of all, I think it will be quite a long time, maybe a hundred years, before we get close to human-level artificial intelligence. I have this opinion from having taught AI as part of my job at San Jose State. The AI field's existing techniques are a handful of cheap parlor tricks.

Second of all, I don't think we'll ever see standalone devices that are vastly more intelligent than people. What we'll see will be intelligence amplification (IA) tools, so that people can create at a higher level. But it'll still be the people doing the creating.

Third, I don't think we'll see injectable nanotech elixirs that can restore a person to a state of youth. I feel that a hysterical fear of death on the part of guys like Ray Kurzweil has clouded the discussions of the Singularity. I think it's lame and juvenile to worry so much about dying. Didn't Ray take his acid in the Sixties like he was supposed to?

Fourth, I think we'll soon be able to create interactive emulations of individual people that I call lifeboxes. The secret for lifeboxes is to use really large databases rather than extreme AI. If you're a writer and a blogger, you're well on the way to having created your lifebox. Singulatarians are, however, obsessed with a much stronger version of the lifebox, that is, with the notion of creating an artificially alive android-like replica of yourself and thereby achieving a kind of immortality. It's not all that well known that I was one of the very first people to present this "uploading" idea in a science fiction novel, that is, in *Software* in 1982.

I have a strong feeling that the conventional notions of a Singularity don't go nearly far enough. A couple of years ago, I got impatient with the prevalent style of hype about the Singularity and, wanting to move past it, I wrote a novel called *Postsingular*. Charles Stross's *Accelerando* helped me see how to write this book. You load on the miracles and keep a straight face.

Postsingular and its sequel *Hylozoic* are based on the idea that gnarly, naturally occurring processes can serve as programmable computations. So you might be gaining information from an air current, or a candle flame, or the rocking branch of a tree, or an eddy in a stream. You might in fact program one of these processes to be an emulation of yourself.

As I was eager to get the ideas of *Postsingular* into circulation, I followed Cory Doctorow's example and released an edition of my book for free online under a Creative Commons license. The release didn't seem to hurt the hardback and paperback sales. But now that e-book sales are finally ramping up, I don't think I'll do CC releases anymore.

For a dude from Kentucky (I'm another), you exhibit a shocking lack of provincialism in your life and work. How come? Has this been a hindrance?

It's a bit of an American tradition to have a rube from the sticks become a cultured cosmopolitan. Harold Ross, the founder of the *New Yorker*, was from Colorado. William Gibson grew up in Wytheville, Virginia.

One reason I learned about more than Louisville was that my mother was from Berlin, and I have a lot of relatives in Germany. We went there several times when I was a boy, and I spent most of the eighth grade in a Black Forest boarding school.

Certainly I was still somewhat provincial when I arrived at Swarthmore College in 1963. But after college I married Sylvia, a Hungarian woman whose family lived in Switzerland, and we ended up visiting them in Europe nearly every year thereafter. And in the U.S., we were of course attending graduate school, working at universities, and culture-vulturing any and all available events.

Speaking of Kentucky, Terry, I always enjoy seeing you at SF events, as you have the feel of a distant cousin from down home. A fellow Kentucky ham, both of us well cured.

I don't get your transrealism thing. Hasn't the novel always been made out of the stuff of the author's life? Is there any other way? Or do you think SF is different?

It's not really the case that every novel is made of the author's life. People very often settle for writing about stock situations, or about scenarios they've encountered in other books or in movies, or about arbitrary things they've completely made up. What impressed me about the Beats when I started reading them in high school was that they were writing about their actual lives—and in a confessional, self-revelatory kind of way.

My notion of transrealism is that, if you're writing SF, and also writing about your life, you can enhance or mutate your experiences in interesting ways. I see the familiar power chords of SF—time travel, antigravity, alternate worlds, telepathy, etc.—as standing for certain kinds of archetypal emotions or experiences. Time travel is memory, flight is enlightenment, alternate worlds symbolize the great variety of individual world-views, and telepathy stands for the ability to communicate fully. If you're using the power chords, but also writing about your life, you end up with something richer than realism and more engaging than sheer fabulation.

Genre fiction like SF is even more at risk of having flat, two-dimensional characters than is normal literary fiction. Perhaps some SF authors imagine that their ideas and situations are so fascinating that they don't need realistic characters. Sticking to a transreal approach is a fairly easy way to ensure that your novel will be lively.

What's the difference between the infinite and the absolute? Do they coexist?

In the branch of mathematics called set theory, infinity is a fairly garden-variety kind of number, and there are lots of different infinities. One is known as alef-null, the size of the set of all natural numbers. Another is called the continuum, and it's the size of the set of all points on a line. My early novel *White Light* is about a young mathematician interested in figuring out the exact relationship between alef-null and the continuum.

The absolute, on the other hand, is more of a philosophical notion. It's the ultimate, inconceivable, largest possible infinity. God, for instance, would be an absolute, and not a mere infinity.

In mathematics, the class of all possible sets is an absolute. There's a semitheological axiom of set theory known as the Reflection Principle. It says that whenever we think we've conceived of the class of all sets, we're thinking of some smaller set. That is, any property enjoyed by the absolute is reflected in the properties of some lower-level infinite set. And any notion you have of God also applies to something smaller. Does that answer your question?

No. What's on your iPhone? What's not on your iPhone?

I have about thirteen gigabytes of music. First I ripped my CDs, then a bunch of CDs from the library, and then I started ripping my old vinyl records, which is an interesting but time-consuming process. You get, I like to think, a richer sound when you digitize the vinyl originals. What kinds of music? Punk rock, Frank Zappa, blues, reggae.

What's not on my iPhone? No books as yet—I'm still holding back from reading digital editions, although just in the last year I've finally started seeing some actual e-book sales on my royalty statements.

Bruce Sterling got me to attend an Augmented Reality (AR) conference in San Jose last year. An example of AR is when you hold up your iPhone and see the world with things overlaid onto it. I got this cool *AR Invaders* app, in which I see UFOs flying around my living room or in the sky over my deck, and I can shoot them. A perfect tool for any SF writer.

Do you think math models the universe? Or the human brain?

Math is the abstract science of form, and seems to be ideally suited for modeling anything at all. It's a universal construction kit. This said, I sometimes feel like the whole idea of science, logic, and math is a little off-the-beam for modeling the universe and the brain. From the inside, life feels like emotion, sounds, colors, and memories, arranged in a mushy and not-particularly-mathematical way.

Our professional organization, SFWA, is currently lobbying Congress to repeal the Scaling Law. Good idea or not?

Terry, you're a card, and sometimes I'm not sure what you're talking about, or if you know either. I'll assume that with the "Scaling Law" you're referring to the empirical fact that society's rewards for creativity are distributed according to an inverse power law—in which an author's financial reward is inversely proportional to his or her popularity.

Rather than lying along a smoothly sloping line, a Scaling Law payment schedule has the form of a violently down-swooping curve, akin to the graph of $1/x$. It's as if society wants to encourage very many books that are precisely of the kind that it likes the most, and to discourage those works that vary in the slightest from the current ideal. The swooping, hyperbolic Scaling Law curve loads money on the best-selling authors, while portioning out much smaller amounts to the scribes out on the long tail.

Disgruntled writers sometimes fantasize about a utopian marketplace in which the Scaling Law distribution would be forcibly replaced by a linear distribution. But this wouldn't work, as I discuss in my nonfiction book *The Lifebox, the Seashell, and the Soul.* Scaling laws are a much a part of nature as are gravitational laws, or the laws of probability. Coming to understand this has greatly helped my serenity—seriously. Sometime math can actually make you happier.

One lesson I can draw from the Scaling Law is that it's okay if my best efforts fail to knock the ball out of the park. There's simply no predicting what's going to catch on, or how big it's going to be. Trying harder isn't going to change anything. Relax, do my work, and don't expect too much. Almost nobody wins, and the winners are effectively chosen at random. Along these lines, the science-fiction writer Marc Laidlaw and I once dreamed of starting a literary movement to be called Freestyle. Our proposed motto: *Write like yourself, only more so.*

A flipside of the Scaling Law is that maintaining even a modest level of success is hard. The gnarly computations of society keep things boiling at every level. As a corollary, note that there's no chance of making things easier for yourself by sending your outputs to lower-paying magazines. They're still likely to reject you, but they'll be ruder and more incompetent about it. Ah me, the writer's life.

You and author Michael Dorris were teenage pals. Did you share any interest in literature, or was it all girls and cars?

I seem to remember that Dorris and I were preoccupied with finding erotic fiction to read, combing the louche bookshops of downtown Louisville. Otherwise our tastes weren't very similar. I recall that he liked James Michener's *Hawaii* and I liked Jean Paul Sartre's *Nausea*. And in the backs of our minds, both of us dreamed of somehow becoming writers. But we didn't talk about it much. I wish very much that he were still alive. Even though he's dead, he's still my friend.

Your novels (and stories, like the ones in this volume) are known for their irreverent and wildly humorous social satire. Why do you hate America?

In the fourth grade I was remanded to a private boys school where I felt bullied and picked upon. And after my college years I had to deal with a government that wanted to draft me and send me to die in a pointless war in Viet Nam. I never fit in well. As I described in my novel *The Secret of Life*, I've always felt like a visiting alien.

Your German grandmother introduced you to the work of Peter Bruegel the Elder at an early age. You later wrote a serious (and wonderful) novel based on his life, As Above, So Below. *Was writing historical fiction a stretch for you?*

In some ways, writing historical fiction is akin to writing fantasy or SF. In each case, you're imagining a complete world that exists in parallel to the world we live in. I considered bringing SF elements into my Bruegel novel, but I decided I didn't want to drag the master into the gutter. His life and times were strange enough on their own.

Something I like about Bruegel's paintings is that sometimes they seem to illustrate a moral or a folk tale, but nobody's ever been able to figure out exactly what the tale is. The Flemish godfather makes you an offer you can't understand. And it's especially the things you can't understand that seem worth knowing.

I remember being very sad when I finished writing *As Above, So Below*. I felt I'd grown very close to Bruegel during my years of work on the book. He'd become like a close friend, or an alter-ego. When the book appeared I was actually living in Bruegel's hometown of Brussels on a grant. His house still stands, and I walked by it in the rain. I felt like Bruegel's ghost was right there with me. He liked my book.

Bruce Sterling once compared the cyberpunk movement (you, Gibson, Cadigan, Shirley, and of course Bruce) to the Beats. Was that accurate? Which were you? (And don't say Kerouac, he had no sense of humor.)

I was William Burroughs—the oldest of the group, rather professorial, and perhaps the gnarliest. In my *Seek!* collection, I have an essay, "Cyberpunk Lives!" that draws this comparison. One of the things I write about in that essay was the time in 1981 when I met Allen Ginsberg in Boulder, Colorado. I asked Allen for his blessing, and he slammed his hand down on the top of my head like the cap of an electric chair, crying out, "Bless you!" It was great. I met Burroughs then, too, but I didn't get very close to him. I managed to give him a copy of novel *White Light*. Bill said, "Far out."

My Jeopardy *topic: SF Today. The answer is, "Because girls just want to have fun." You provide the question.*

Why is supernatural romance so popular?

Do you like guns?

Guns aren't for me. If I kept a gun in my house, I probably would have shot someone by now, possibly myself.

How did you learn to paint? Did it involve unlearning something as well?

In 1999, my wife and I took an oil-painting class in night school at the local museum. I took to it right away.

My level of manual control is low enough that I tend to surprise myself with what I end up painting. Sometimes these surprises show me things that are a good fit for the novel or story that I'm currently working on—you might say that I'm channeling information from another part of my brain. But it's fine if I don't use the images in my fiction. The main thing is that I'm feeding my soul and getting into the moment and, if I'm lucky, turning off my inner monologue. Given that painting doesn't involve words at all, it's even more meditative than writing. I love the luscious colors.

Painting has taught me a few practical things about writing. When I'm doing a painting, for instance, it's not unusual to completely paint over some screwed-up patch and do that part over. I think this has made me feel more relaxed about revising my fiction. And I've also noticed that the details that I haven't yet visualized are the ones that give me the most trouble. But the only way to proceed is to put it down wrong, and then keep changing it until it works.

If there's anything I needed to unlearn, it was the belief that I needed to paint human figures with complete accuracy. Approximations are fine, and I can brush away at a given figure until it looks reasonably okay. We have cameras for accuracy.

"Your soul isn't in fact immortal on its own, but is, rather, a pattern of information that God stores in His memory so that He can resurrect you." Explain.

In the Passion scene in the Gospel according to Luke, the Good Thief says, "Lord, remember me when you come into your kingdom." And Jesus seems to agree with that, and says, "Verily I say unto you, today you will be with me in paradise."

I once had an interesting discussion of this passage with my old science-writer mentor, Martin Gardner. Some religious sects have taken the exchange between Jesus and the Good Thief to mean that your soul isn't in fact immortal on its own, but is, rather, a pattern of information that God stores in memory so as to resurrect you. Sometimes the word "soul sleep" is associated with this notion.

Keeping it simple, to me the Thief/Jesus exchange suggests that the soul can in fact be represented as software, that is, as a pattern of information that God (or a sufficiently large computer memory) can store.

Of course, realistically speaking, when it comes to immortality, we're grasping at straws. These days I'm more inclined to think that it's going to be a matter of lights-out and that's all she wrote. That used to bother me, but now it seems okay. I think when you're younger you're concerned about living long enough to do things you feel you need to do. But I've been lucky, and by now I've pretty much checked off everything on my list. Not that I wouldn't mind another twenty years.

Your work describes a universe in which anything can happen and often does. Is this a literary device, or wishful thinking?

One reason I write is so I can travel out of my ordinary world. I like running with any crazy idea that pops into my head, fleshing it out and giving it substance. I really do feel that there are some as yet unsuspected levels of reality, and SF can help us find our way there.

There's a kind of transreal aspect too. When I write a novel, I am to some extent leaving this world and going into another one—the world of the novel. So it's natural that in my novel, the main character leaves his or her world and goes off into some other dimension or alternate reality. Because that's exactly what I'm doing by writing the book.

BIBLIOGRAPHY

BOOKS

Jim and the Flims, SF novel, Night Shade Books, 2011.

Nested Scrolls, PS Publishing and Tor Books, 2011.

The Ware Tetralogy, omnibus edition of *Software, Wetware, Freeware, and Realware*, Prime Books, 2010.

Hylozoic, SF novel (sequel to *Postsingular*), Tor Books, 2009.

Postsingular, SF novel, Tor Books, 2007.

Mad Professor, collected SF stories, Thunder's Mouth Press, 2007.

Mathematicians in Love, SF novel, Tor Books, 2006.

The Lifebox, the Seashell, and the Soul, nonfiction on computers and reality, Thunder's Mouth Press 2005; Basic Books, 2006.

Frek and the Elixir, SF novel, Tor Books, 2004.

Software Engineering and Computer Games, textbook, Addison-Wesley, 2003.

Spaceland, SF novel, Tor Books, 2002.

As Above, So Below: A Novel of Peter Bruegel, historical novel, Forge Books, 2002.

Gnarl! collected SF stories, Four Walls Eight Windows, 2000.

Realware, SF novel, Avon Books, 2000.

Saucer Wisdom, SF novel, Forge Books, 1999.

Seek!, collected essays, Four Walls Eight Windows, 1999.

Freeware, SF novel, Avon Books, 1997.

The Hacker and the Ants, SF novel, Avon Books 1994; Four Walls Eight Windows, 2002.

Transreal!, collected poems, SF stories, and essays, WCS Books, 1991.

All The Visions, memoir, Ocean View Books, 1991.

The Hollow Earth, SF novel, William Morrow & Co., 1990; Avon Books, 1992; Monkeybrain Books, 2008.

Wetware, SF novel, Avon Books, 1988, Avon Books, 1997.

Mind Tools, nonfiction on mathematics and information, Houghton Mifflin, 1987.

The Secret of Life, SF novel, Bluejay Books, 1985; ElectricStory, 2001.

Master of Space and Time, SF novel, Bluejay Books, 1984; Baen Books, 1985; Running Press, 2005.

The Fourth Dimension, nonfiction, Houghton Mifflin, 1984.

Light Fuse and Get Away, self-published poetry chapbook, Carp Press, 1983.

The Sex Sphere, SF novel, Ace Books, 1983; E-Reads, 2008.

The Fifty-Seventh Franz Kafka, collected SF stories, Ace Books, 1983.

Software, SF novel, Ace Books 1982; Avon Books, 1987; Avon Books, 1997.

Infinity and the Mind, nonfiction, Birkhäuser, 1982; Bantam. 1983; Princeton University Press, 1995, 2005.

Spacetime Donuts, SF novel, Ace Books 1981; E-Reads, 2008.

White Light, SF novel, Ace Books 1980; Wired Books 1997; Four Walls Eight Windows, 2001.

Geometry, Relativity and the Fourth Dimension, nonfiction, Dover, 1977.

BOOKS EDITED

MONDO 2000: A User's Guide to the New Edge, HarperCollins, 1992 (with R.U. Sirius and Queen Mu).

Semiotext(e) SF, Autonomedia, 1989 (with Peter Wilson and Robert Anton Wilson).

Mathenauts: Tales of Mathematical Wonder, Arbor House, 1987.

Speculations on the Fourth Dimension: Selected Writings of Charles Howard Hinton, Dover, 1983.

SOFTWARE PACKAGES

The Pop Game Framework, San Jose State University, 2003.

CAPOW, San Jose State University, 1998 (with a team of students).

Artificial Life Lab, Waite Group Press, 1993.

CHAOS: James Gleick's Chaos Software, Autodesk, 1990 (with Josh Gordon and John Walker).

CA Lab: Rudy Rucker's Cellular Automata Laboratory, Autodesk, 1989 (with John Walker).

ABOUT THE AUTHOR

ONE OF THE ORIGINAL DREAD LORDS of science fiction's cyberpunk movement, Rudolf von Bitter Rucker is the great-great-great-grandson of philosopher G.W.F. Hegel.

Since his incarnation in 1946, Rucker has been a mathematician, science author (*The Fourth Dimension*), online editor (*Flurb*), award-winning SF writer (two Philip K. Dick Awards for his *Ware* novels) and an old-school computer hacker.

He also paints.

A native of Kentucky, he lives in Silicon Valley with his wife, a Hungarian beauty.

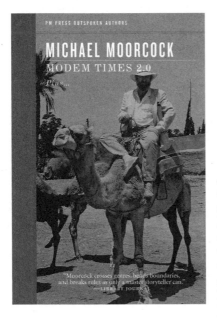

PM PRESS
OUTSPOKEN AUTHORS

Modem Times 2.0
Michael Moorcock
978-1-60486-308-6
$12

As the editor of London's revolutionary *New Worlds* magazine in the swinging sixties, Michael Moorcock has been credited with virtually inventing modern Science Fiction: publishing such figures as Norman Spinrad, Samuel R. Delany, Brian Aldiss and J.G. Ballard.

Moorcock's own literary accomplishments include his classic "Mother London," a romp through urban history conducted by psychic outsiders; his comic Pyat Quartet, in which a Jewish antisemite examines the roots of the Nazi Holocaust; *Behold the Man*, the tale of a time tourist who fills in for Christ on the cross; and of course the eternal hero Elric, swordswinger, hellbringer and bestseller.

And now Moorcock's most audacious creation, Jerry Cornelius—assassin, rock star, chronospy and maybe-Messiah—is back in *Modem Times 2.0*, a time twisting odyssey that connects 60s London with post-Obama America, with stops in Palm Springs and Guantanamo. *Modem Times 2.0* is Moorcock at his most outrageously readable—a masterful mix of erudition and subversion.

Plus: a non-fiction romp in the spirit of Swift and Orwell, "My Londons"; and an Outspoken Interview with literature's authentic Lord of Misrule.

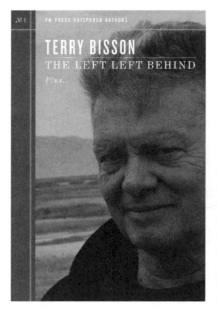

PM PRESS OUTSPOKEN AUTHORS

The Left Left Behind
Terry Bisson
978-1-60486-086-3
$12

Hugo and Nebula award-winner Terry Bisson is best known for his short stories, which range from the southern sweetness of "Bears Discover Fire" to the alienated aliens of "They're Made out of Meat." He is also a 1960s New Left vet with a history of activism and an intact (if battered) radical ideology.

The *Left Behind* novels (about the so-called "Rapture" in which all the born-agains ascend straight to heaven) are among the bestselling Christian books in the U.S., describing in lurid detail the adventures of those "left behind" to battle the Anti-Christ. Put Bisson and the Born-Agains together, and what do you get? *The Left Left Behind*—a sardonic, merciless, tasteless, take-no-prisoners satire of the entire apocalyptic enterprise that spares no one-predatory preachers, goth lingerie, Pacifica radio, Indian casinos, gangsta rap, and even "art cars" at Burning Man.

Plus: "Special Relativity," a one-act drama that answers the question: When Albert Einstein, Paul Robeson, J. Edgar Hoover are raised from the dead at an anti-Bush rally, which one wears the dress? As with all Outspoken Author books, there is a deep interview and autobiography: at length, in-depth, no-holds-barred, and all-bets-off: an extended tour though the mind and work, the history and politics of our Outspoken Author. Surprises are promised.

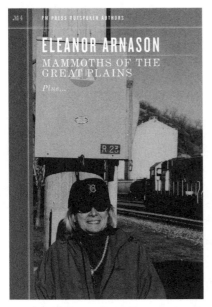

PM PRESS
OUTSPOKEN AUTHORS

Mammoths of the Great Plains
Eleanor Arnason
978-1-60486-075-7
$12

When President Thomas Jefferson sent Lewis and Clark to explore the West, he told them to look especially for mammoths. Jefferson had seen bones and tusks of the great beasts in Virginia, and he suspected—he hoped!—that they might still roam the Great Plains. In Eleanor Arnason's imaginative alternate history, they do: shaggy herds thunder over the grasslands, living symbols of the oncoming struggle between the Native peoples and the European invaders. And in an unforgettable saga that soars from the badlands of the Dakotas to the icy wastes of Siberia, from the Russian Revolution to the AIM protests of the 1960s, Arnason tells of a modern woman's struggle to use the weapons of DNA science to fulfill the ancient promises of her Lakota heritage.

Plus: "Writing SF During World War III," and an Outspoken Interview that takes you straight into the heart and mind of one of today's edgiest and most uncompromising speculative authors.

Praise:
"Eleanor Arnason nudges both human and natural history around so gently in this tale that you hardly know you're not in the world-as-we-know-it until you're quite at home in a North Dakota where you've never been before, listening to your grandmother tell you the world."   —Ursula K. Le Guin

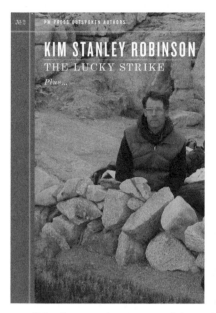

PM PRESS
OUTSPOKEN AUTHORS

The Lucky Strike
Kim Stanley Robinson
978-1-60486-085-6
$12

Combining dazzling speculation with a profoundly humanist vision, Kim Stanley Robinson is known as not only the most literary but also the most progressive (read "radical") of today's top-rank SF authors. His bestselling Mars Trilogy tells the epic story of the future colonization of the red planet, and the revolution that inevitably follows. His latest novel, *Galileo's Dream*, is a stunning combination of historical drama and far-flung space opera, in which the ten dimensions of the universe itself are rewoven to ensnare history's most notorious torturers.

The Lucky Strike, the classic and controversial story Robinson has chosen for PM's new Outspoken Authors series, begins on a lonely Pacific island, where a crew of untested men are about to take off in an untried aircraft with a deadly payload that will change our world forever. Until something goes wonderfully wrong.

Plus: *A Sensitive Dependence on Initial Conditions*, in which Robinson dramatically deconstructs "alternate history" to explore what might have been if things had gone differently over Hiroshima that day.

As with all Outspoken Author books, there is a deep interview and autobiography: at length, in-depth, no-holds-barred and all-bets-off: an extended tour though the mind and work, the history and politics of our Outspoken Author. Surprises are promised.

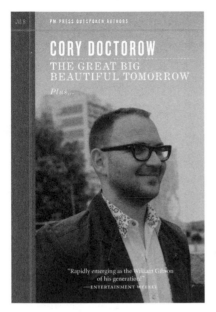

PM PRESS OUTSPOKEN AUTHORS

The Great Big Beautiful Tomorrow
Cory Doctorow
978-1-60486-404-5
$12

Cory Doctorow burst on the SF scene in 2000 like a rocket, inspiring awe in readers (and envy in other writers) with his bestselling novels and stories, which he insisted on giving away via Creative Commons. Meanwhile, as coeditor of the wildly popular Boing Boing, he became the radical new voice of the Web, boldly arguing for internet freedom from corporate control.

Doctorow's activism and artistry are both on display in this Outspoken Author edition. The crown jewel is his novella, *The Great Big Beautiful Tomorrow*—the high-velocity adventures of a trans-human teenager in a post-Disney dystopia, battling wireheads and wumpuses (and having fun doing it!) until he meets the "meat girl" of his dreams, and is forced to choose between immortality and sex.

Plus a live transcription of Cory's historic address to the 2010 World SF Convention, "Creativity vs. Copyright," dramatically presenting his controversial case for open-source in both information and art. Also included is an international Outspoken Interview in which Doctorow reveals the surprising sources of his genius.

FRIENDS OF

These are indisputably momentous times – the financial system is melting down globally and the Empire is stumbling. Now more than ever there is a vital need for radical ideas.

In the four years since its founding—and on a mere shoestring—PM Press has risen to the formidable challenge of publishing and distributing knowledge and entertainment for the struggles ahead. With over 175 releases to date, we have published an impressive and stimulating array of literature, art, music, politics, and culture. Using every available medium, we've succeeded in connecting those hungry for ideas and information to those putting them into practice.

Friends of PM allows you to directly help impact, amplify, and revitalize the discourse and actions of radical writers, filmmakers, and artists. It provides us with a stable foundation from which we can build upon our early successes and provides a much-needed subsidy for the materials that can't necessarily pay their own way. You can help make that happen —and receive every new title automatically delivered to your door once a month—by joining as a Friend of PM Press. And, we'll throw in a free T-Shirt when you sign up.

Here are your options:

• $25 a month: Get all books and pamphlets plus 50% discount on all webstore purchases

• $40 a month: Get all PM Press releases (including CDs and DVDs) plus 50% discount on all webstore purchases

• $100 a month: Superstar—Everything plus PM merchandise, free downloads, and 50% discount on all webstore purchases

For those who can't afford $25 or more a month, we're introducing Sustainer Rates at $15, $10 and $5. Sustainers get a free PM Press t-shirt and a 50% discount on all purchases from our website.

Your Visa or Mastercard will be billed once a month, until you tell us to stop. Or until our efforts succeed in bringing the revolution around. Or the financial meltdown of Capital makes plastic redundant. Whichever comes first.

PM PRESS was founded at the end of 2007 by a small collection of folks with decades of publishing, media, and organizing experience. PM Press co-conspirators have published and distributed hundreds of books, pamphlets, CDs, and DVDs. Members of PM have founded enduring book fairs, spearheaded victorious tenant organizing campaigns, and worked closely with bookstores, academic conferences, and even rock bands to deliver political and challenging ideas to all walks of life. We're old enough to know what we're doing and young enough to know what's at stake.

We seek to create radical and stimulating fiction and non-fiction books, pamphlets, t-shirts, visual and audio materials to entertain, educate and inspire you. We aim to distribute these through every available channel with every available technology—whether that means you are seeing anarchist classics at our bookfair stalls; reading our latest vegan cookbook at the café; downloading geeky fiction e-books; or digging new music and timely videos from our website.

PM Press is always on the lookout for talented and skilled volunteers, artists, activists and writers to work with. If you have a great idea for a project or can contribute in some way, please get in touch.

PM PRESS
PO Box 23912
Oakland CA 94623
510-658-3906
www.pmpress.org